THE SILVER CHANTER
Traditional Scottish Tales & Legends

This invigorating collection of Scottish stories comprises some remembered from Wendy Wood's own childhood, others by Highland friends, and all a testimony of her lifelong devotion to Scotland. So gifted a storyteller is Wendy Wood that well-known legends and lesser-known stories alike take on a special magic in her hands. Whether about heroes, giants and princesses in possession of magical powers, or ordinary people caught up with the supernatural, Wendy Wood's stories are always infused by her great love of all things Scottish, and unerringly capture the couthy Scots tongue and musical rhythm of the Gaelic.

The
Silver Chanter

Traditional Scottish Tales and Legends

By

WENDY WOOD

Illustrated by
COLIN McNAUGHTON

CHATTO & WINDUS · LONDON

Published by
Chatto & Windus Ltd.
40 William IV Street
London WC2N 4DF

*

Clarke, Irwin & Co. Ltd.,
Toronto

British Library Cataloguing in Publication Data
Wood, Wendy
        The silver chanter
        1. Tales, Scottish
        2. Legends, Scottish
        I. Title
        398.2'09411   GR144

    ISBN 0-7011-2448 2

Printed and bound in Great Britain by
Redwood Burn Ltd
Trowbridge and Esher

CONTENTS

THE SILVER CHANTER

1. Thomas Rymer

It was market day at Ercildoune (now the village of Earlston in the Borders) and what a noise! Cattle moo-ing, sheep baa-ing, children running around shrieking, dogs barking, and men shouting. But no one was shouting louder than Thomas Rymer.

"Look at my cattle," he yelled, "the best in all Scotland. See their glossy coats, their fat sides, their lovely horns." Everyone near him laughed, for though Thomas had a good farm, he was lazy; he liked telling jokes to make people laugh, he liked to play his lute and sing. Soon on this market day he was doing this, laughing and joking and singing the praises of the lassies. Thomas did not even seem to mind very much when at evening he had to tell his drover to take back his cattle unsold.

Later that week, he sat under a great thorn tree at the edge of a wood, playing his lute and making new songs, but

9

he grew tired, the scent of the may blossom made him drowsy, and anyway, he thought the birds were making better music than himself, so he set his instrument aside. It was then that he heard the sound of tiny bells, and he wondered at so sweet a sound. Where could it come from? Then he saw a white horse coming out of the wood, ridden by a lady so beautiful that he had never been able to imagine anyone so lovely. Her green dress shimmered with light.

"You must be the Queen of Heaven," he whispered.

"No, Thomas," she said, "but I am the Queen of the Otherworld, which some call 'faerie'. I heard you singing. Will you sing again for me? I could listen to you for ever." Thomas sang again and she was so pleased.

"I wish you could come and live with me," she said. This was just what Thomas wanted to do, and he asked for a kiss.

"No," she said, "for if you kiss me, you will have to come with me and stay for seven years."

"Oh yes, I'll come," said Thomas quickly.

"But," said the Queen, "in all those years you mustn't speak. You must not say *one* word, or you will never be able to return home, never see your farm again, or your friends." But Thomas did not care, and they kissed.

"Now you must go with me," she said, and told him to mount the horse behind her. Immediately away they went, the silver bells on the horse's mane tinkling as they sped faster than the wind over mountains and moors, over forests and fields. When they came to the Otherworld, he was given silken clothes and fine food and drink, so he never needed to ask for anything, but just served the Queen and was completely happy for seven years. Then the Queen came to him.

"Seven years are past, Thomas. You must return home."

"Oh no," said Thomas, greatly distressed. "I don't think I have been here more than three days. I have kept my promise not to speak, and I will do anything to stay with you."

10

"You must go today," she said sadly, "but some day I will send for you. Come now, I have something special to give you." She took him to an orchard where the trees were loaded down with lovely fruits, and picked an apple for him. "Eat this," she said, "and you will always speak the truth." Thomas had nearly taken a bite, but he hesitated.

"I don't think I *want* to always speak the truth," he said. "You see, if I spoke the truth on market day about my cattle, nobody would buy them, and when I make songs about the girls, I compliment them even if they are not bonny. I couldn't disappoint and offend them by saying what they really look like."

"But," said the Queen, "you will be able to tell the truth about things that have not yet happened, and that will make you famous all over the land, and it will make you rich too, for many will seek you for your knowledge of what is going to happen." This seemed like sense so Thomas ate the apple. With a sigh he again mounted the horse behind the Queen, and with a tinkling of silver bells, away they went over mountains and moors, over fields and forests, on and on, till they arrived back at the great thorn tree, and there she left him.

Thomas returned sadly to his farm and went next day with his cattle to the market. The people crowded round him expecting him to boast as usual about his cattle, but he set them all laughing when he shouted, "Look at my cattle! Did you ever see such poor beasts? They are thin and their coats are dirty, their horns are no more than bumps, and two of them are lame and can scarcely walk."

"Thomas is speaking the truth!" they cried, and some bought a beast or two for, "We are not being cheated" they said, "and we will get them at a low price and can fatten them."

The girls wanted as usual to hear his pretty compliments and gave him drinks and kisses, but they were insulted and very angry when he sang that Betty had squint eyes, and

Bella's hair which he had always described as "golden", he now called "straw". Thomas went home very unhappy and wished he had never tasted that apple.

The next week, he was sitting with some of his companions, when he suddenly started to moan and say, "Woe, woe for Scotland, for by this time tomorrow the King of Scots will be dead. Never did we have so good a King, who brought happiness to all his people, woe, woe that tomorrow we will have no King." Everyone was shocked, they thought he must really be mad.

"Indeed," they rebuked him, "it's wicked to say such things, and as the King is not even ill, what can happen to him? We hear he is leaving the Court to visit his Queen, so what you say is nonsense," and they took no more notice.

But the next day, as the King was riding across Fife to see his wife at Perth, a great mist came down and he could not see his way. He did not know that he was on the edge of cliffs that had started to crumble. The horse stumbled, the edge gave way, and they both fell crashing to the rocks below and were killed.

Then the people wondered how their friend Thomas had known beforehand that it would happen. "We didn't believe him," they said, "but he was right."

Thomas began to know a lot of things that would happen. He knew of battles to come, who would win, and who would lose, and he said of the family of Haig that lived at Bermyside,

> "Betide, betide, what e'er betide
> Haig shall be Haig of Bemerside."

This statement really made them laugh, for the Haig family had twelve daughters who could not inherit the estate, and the mother was too old to have more children. Yet that year she gave birth to a son, and the Haigs have been in Bemerside ever since.

A more useful purpose for which Thomas could use his

talent was foretelling the weather, and many a farmer paid him for such information. Soon nobles were coming from the Court to consult him and pay him a lot of money for what he could tell them. In this way he became very rich, as the Faerie Queen had promised.

Having so much money, he built a castle for himself, and because he was not selfish, he gave a great feast at his castle for rich and poor alike. The great hall was filled with tables spread with unlimited dishes of food and goblets of wine. Entertainers showed tame bears, there were wrestling contests and much dancing and singing, though Thomas did neither for he was sadly thinking of his lovely Queen, and longing to be with her again.

Just then a laddie ran into the hall and whispered to Thomas, "There is a white hind coming up the road towards the castle." Thomas went to the door, and there, surely enough, a white hind, looking silver in the moonlight, was waiting for him. He put his arm round its neck and they passed slowly together away from the castle, away from Ercildoune into the wood, and were never seen again.

"He will come back," the people assured themselves, "he was away before this and returned, he will come back some day." But Thomas Rymer has not done so — not yet.

2. The Wee Bannock

Jock came in hungry from making hay, and was glad to see that his wife had two round oatmeal bannocks toasting at the fire, a big one and a little one.

"That's good," he said, and grabbed the big one, breaking it and starting to eat.

The Wee Bannock did not like this. "It's time I was away," it thought. "I'll get out before that happens to me," and it jumped from the fireside and bowled away under the table.

"Ho!" cried the wife, "look at yon Wee Bannock, it's away. Grup it, Jock, grup it!" But the Wee Bannock jinked this way and that, round the water bucket, under the dresser and away out of the door. It ran to the next house, thinking it would have a nice quiet warm at the fire. But a tailor was sitting at the hearth with his big pressing-iron in his hand.

14

THE WEE BANNOCK

"Heh! I see a Wee Bannock," he shouted to his wife. "Grup it, wife, grup it!" She threw a porridge spurtle[1] at it, and he threw the iron, but they both missed; indeed the porridge spurtle accidentally hit her on the head and the iron landed on her toes.

"Ouch! You muckle gowk[2]!" she shouted, and scratched his face.

"Catch the bannock, ye gomeril[3]," he yelled, "grup it! Grup it!" But the Wee Bannock jinked this way and that, under the ironing board, round their feet, against his plaid and away out of the door to the next house, where a woman was turning the handle of a churn making butter.

"Eh! A Wee Bannock," she said, "just the thing with a pat of butter," and she put out her hand to catch it, but the Wee Bannock jinked this way and that, and she dashed about after it till she tripped and nearly cowped[4] the churn.

"Ye wee divvil," she shouted, and threw her shoe at it, but missed, and the Wee Bannock spun out of the door and down the hill to the Mill. The miller was just emptying some flour from a sack.

"Eh! A Wee Bannock," he said, "that's good luck, and just the thing with a mug of ale for supper," and he made a grab, but the Wee Bannock rolled under the sack, and over the mill-stone, and jinked this way and that. The miller flung his cap at it, but missed, and the Wee Bannock was away out of the door to the next house, which was a farm.

"I'll be snug and safe here," it said. Three men were sitting round the fire talking to the farmer and his wife, and drinking beer.

"I see a Wee Bannock," said one.

"Just the thing to go with ale," said another, "grup it, grup it!" They all got up to the chase and the Wee Bannock

[1] stick for stirring porridge   [2] fool
[3] idiot   [4] upset

15

jinked this way and that. "Grup it!" they shouted, falling over the furniture and knocking each other down.

"Dear me," thought the Wee Bannock, "this is no place for me," and spun away out of the door. It was getting dark when it reached the next house, and the couple were going to bed. The man was just taking off his trousers, when he saw the Wee Bannock come in.

"Ho ho!" he said, "I telt ye, ye gave me a gey[1] skimpy supper, but here's a Wee Bannock, half for me and half for you if you catch it. Grup it, wife, grup it!" he shouted. The wife threw first one shoe and then another at the Wee Bannock and missed.

"Grup it yourself!" she cried, and flung the pillow, which burst, and the air was full of feathers that made them choke. "Grup it!" she shouted at her husband, "quick, it's going out of the door." So it was, and the man chased it, throwing his trousers after it, but the Wee Bannock jinked here and there and won away, and the man went home terribly ashamed to be half naked.

It was dark now, and the Wee Bannock was very tired. It found a nice cosy fox's hole under a whin bush and went to sleep. But the fox had been out hunting and had caught nothing, so it was pleased to find a nice bannock.

"A lovely supper," he said, and gobbled it up, and that was the end of the Wee Bannock.

[1] very

16

3. The Silver Chanter

Iain sat on the meal-bin kicking his heels. He was the youngest of the MacCrimmon boys, being only eight years old, while Colin and Peter were fourteen and sixteen, and both of them good pipers. Iain had reason to be annoyed, for his father and the two elder ones were away to the market to sell some cattle. Iain was thinking how interesting and what fun it would be at the market. Everyone in the village would be out and about in the little street, or giving drinks in their cottages to the visitors. All sorts of cattle would be roaring in the pens; sheep all over the place being steered by barking collies. There would be women selling butter and sweets (Iain's mouth watered at the thought) and men selling home-made shoes (he could do with another pair for there was a hole in the toe of one of his brogues) and above all there would be many pipers — including his father and two brothers.

Iain longed to be a good piper, but the fact was, that every time he tried to play, his brothers would cover their ears, and his father say,

"For goodness sake, Iain, stop that row, it's like a herd of mad cats. You'll never make a piper." But Iain went on trying.

Today, alone on the croft, he was supposed to be looking after the cattle. Well, they were grazing down by the shore and he thought he had better go and have a look at them, but he would take the pipes. Yes, he would try once again. Down on the shore the cattle were all right, so Iain walked around trying to play. The result was awful. Iain knew it was awful.

"I'll NEVER be a piper," he said sadly to himself. He put down the pipes, and sitting beside a cave, he watched the cows and the tide lapping on the shore.

"I wish I could be a really good piper," he said.

"So you *could*," said a voice, and looking round, he saw it was a little old lady who had spoken. He was very surprised, because he had never seen her before, and yet he knew everyone in the glen and round about.

"How could I be a good piper?" he asked wonderingly. "I know I'm awful."

"Yes, you are, but perhaps I can teach you if you will do as I say."

"I'll do *anything* you tell me," said Iain eagerly.

"Well," said the woman, "this cave is called 'Uamha an Oir', the cave of gold, and I could give you as much gold as would buy you anything you want. I could make you a rich man for life — or I could make you the best piper in all Scotland. Which would you rather be, so very rich or a good piper?"

Iain thought of what he could give to his father: more cattle, a new boat, and for his brothers and himself, new clothes, new shoes, fishing tackle, perhaps a horse to ride, but he would rather be a really good piper. To pipe so that people would not be able to help dancing; to pipe so that the sound told the history of Scotland; to pipe sadness so that people would weep; to pipe gaiety that brought laughter.

"I'd rather be a really good piper," he said solemnly.

"Then do as I tell you, Iain. Throw that black chanter from you into the sea."

"Oh no, I can't do that! How can I play without a chanter? I put a new reed in only yesterday."

"Do as I tell you." So Iain disconnected the chanter from his set and threw it into the sea. It bobbed about for a minute and then disappeared. He felt dreadful. Pipes and no chanter! It would have been better to have had a chanter and no pipes, for he could still have practised. He began to think the nasty old woman was playing a trick on him, but she was handing him another chanter, and it was not made of wood, but of silver.

"Now," she said, "think of *any* tune you want to play, and you will be able to play it."

"She's crazy," said Iain to himself. But he thought he would try a stirring march. He stood up and filled the bag, tuned the pipes and strode along the shore, the great sounds pealing across the land. His whole being was just one great bursting happiness as the bag filled and refilled and his nimble fingers found the notes.

"You see," said the old woman, "you are now the greatest piper in Scotland, you're the King of Pipers — but — you must remember that the Silver Chanter must always be treated with the greatest respect. Never must a word be said against it."

"Of course," said Iain excitedly, "and I thank you, oh *how* I thank you," but the old woman was not there to be thanked, she had vanished. Iain realised by the position of the sun that it was evening, and his father and brothers would be returning, so he gathered the cows, and following them towards the cottage he strode and played, no one in

19

all Scotland happier than he; nor did he stop playing when he got home, no indeed, to and fro before the house he swaggered, playing away.

His father and brothers heard the sound a long way off.

"Who can that be playing the pipes?" they asked each other.

"That is the greatest piper I have ever heard," said the father, and soon they were so excited at the wonderful piping, that they began to run. When they saw it was Iain, they were absolutely dumbfounded. They made him tell all about the old woman and asked him to play again and again, and whatever tune they asked for, he could play.

So Iain, being the best piper in all Scotland, went about the land teaching, and he and his descendants became pipers to the Chiefs of the Clan MacLeod. Generations later, Iain's great-great-grandson was accompanying the Chief on a sea voyage when a great storm blew up. Huge green waves topped with spray heaved the boat up as if it climbed mountains and then dropped it into deep curving troughs. The sails were whipped to shreds, the white foam rushed alongside like torn lace. No wonder the piper was seasick! But the crew, who were used to the sea, mocked the piper.

"What sort of piping is that? A tinker could do better," they teased.

"It's this stupid chanter," the piper shouted in a moment of fury. He had forgotten about the faerie woman who had taught his great-great-grandfather Iain, and that she had warned never to speak disrespectfully of the chanter. "It's this good-for-nothing chanter!" he shouted again, and was horrified when it slipped from his hand and fell into the sea.

After that the MacCrimmons lost the greatness of their playing, but people remembered it and made a song and a pipe tune which they called 'Cha till MacCrimmon' (Mac-Crimmon will never return). One day a young MacCrimmon piper said he would go into the cave where Iain had seen the old woman, hoping to find her again and perhaps get another silver chanter. It was a deep cave, and his friends and relations begged him not to go.

"You will not find her, and even if you do, she may be angry and will do you harm," they warned him. But the young piper was determined. They watched him tucking the bag under his arm and march playing into the cave. The sound was strange in the restricted space, and got less and less, till only a few could hear it. Then there was silence; complete silence. They waited, expecting to hear the sound of the pipes returning. They waited till evening, indeed some waited all night, but still there was only the sound of the waves and the wind in the mouth of the cave. The piper never came back, but they say that sometimes, on the hill above Uamha ar Oir, you can still hear the sound of the pipes.

4. Tamlinn

Tamlinn's father had been killed in battle, but he was very lucky because the Earl of Roxburgh had adopted him, and treated him as his son, teaching him the arts of arms and riding, and Tam was very proud the day that he was allowed to join the hunting party in the woods of Carterhaugh. He was only nine years old and the horse was rather big for him, but it had been chosen because it was quiet and it lagged behind the other riders. The deer they had been hunting had got away, and the nobles had hurried home to have a meal, so the woods were silent; the young rider was tired and dozed, indeed he soon slept, and slid out of the saddle on to the soft forest ground without interrupting his sleep.

When he wakened, he found himself among the faeries who were known to live in Carterhaugh woods. The Elf Queen thought him a lovely lad, and put a spell on him that made him half-faerie so that he would have to stay with her for ever.

Not far away was the Castle of Oakwood where Mr. Scott lived with his daughter Janet. She was a bonny lass and her father was troubled that she did not seem to want to marry. Truth to tell, Janet was bored; she longed for adventure instead of sewing and reading and playing chess with her father, and as she looked at the woods of Carterhaugh from her little bedroom window, she thought how nice it would be to wander in them, the more so, as girls were warned not to go there because they might meet the young faerie Knight Tamlinn who had sometimes been seen riding there. This warning made Janet want to go into the woods more than ever, and on the evening of Midsummer she was determined to venture.

So after supper she slipped out of the castle and went into the woods. They were just as lovely as she had expected, and she was fascinated by the beauty of the wild roses that grew there, particularly a bush of white ones that had an almost magic perfume. She was picking some when she noticed a riderless horse grazing nearby. Thinking that the rider must return, Janet stayed to watch. She was not disappointed, for the youth who returned to his horse was the most handsome she had ever seen, so she was surprised when he asked her crossly: "How *dare* you pluck the roses of Carterhaugh woods?"

"Why shouldn't I?" demanded Janet, not in the least afraid and not used to being spoken to so severely.

"I am Tamlinn," he said, "and the Elf Queen has made me guardian of these woods."

"Oh! So you are Tamlinn who lives with the faeries!"

"The Queen put a spell on me when I was nine years old. I am her special knight, and she will not let me return to be mortal again."

"Do you want to be?" queried Janet. "I should have thought it must be wonderful to be of her Court."

"When I see you," said Tamlinn, "I long to be mortal again."

"What prevents you?"

"A terrible trouble prevents me," said Tamlinn, looking sad. "I can only become mortal again if someone loves me enough to break the spell and that would be horribly dangerous, and must be done at midnight tonight because it is Midsummer night."

"What is it? I will do it," said Janet eagerly.

"It would need a very, very brave person to do it," said Tamlinn.

"I am brave," boasted Janet. "I am not afraid of anything, and I want so very much to set you free of the spell and make you mortal again."

"Well," said Tamlinn, "you would need to be here at midnight exactly, and you will then see the Queen and her Court ride through the woods. First you will see the Elf Queen and her company approach, led by a knight on a black horse. You must be hidden, quiet and still, and let them go by.

"Then you will see a second company approach led by a knight on a brown horse. You must stay hidden, quiet and still, and let him go by.

"Then you will see a third company approach, which I will be leading on a white horse, and you will also know me by the gold circlet on my head."

"What must I do then?" asked Janet excitedly.

"You must rush out and seize my horse's reins, pull me from the saddle, wrap your arms round me and hold me tight. If you let go, I will have to remain with the Queen for ever."

"I will do as you say," said Janet with great determination, but she did not have the least idea how difficult that was going to be. She went back to the Castle and went to bed, and just before twelve o'clock, when everyone else was sleeping, she crept down the stone stairs, opened the creaking door and slipped outside.

The woods looked mysterious in the moonlight, an owl hooted and Janet felt afraid, but she thought of Tamlinn and went on to hide behind a bush as he had told her. It was so silent, so eerie; there was a cold little wind, she trembled as she drew her plaid closer round her shoulders. At last she heard the light sound of horses galloping, and saw the first company approaching with the Queen in their midst, and led by a knight on a black horse. She stayed hidden, kept perfectly still, and let them go by. Soon after, a second company of faeries approached, led by a knight on a brown horse. She stayed hidden, kept perfectly quiet and still, and let them go by. Silence again. Then she heard the sound of horses' hoofs again, and the third company approached, led by Tamlinn on a white horse, the moonlight shining on the gold circlet on his head, and Janet rushed out, pulled him from the saddle and held him fast in her arms.

But the Elf Queen had seen, and was so angry that she cast a spell, and turned Tamlinn into a large ugly lizard, and Janet might well have let go, but she held on. That made the Queen angrier than ever, and she turned the lizard into a huge slimy snake that curled round Janet's neck and almost throttled her — but still she held on. Then the Queen was furious and turned the snake into a bar of red hot iron that burnt Janet's hands till she could hardly bear it, but she held on. The Elf Queen then realised that Janet's love was greater than any spells, and the bar of iron turned into Tamlinn again.

"Alas!" cried the Queen. "I have lost the bonniest knight I have ever had! Farewell, Tamlinn!" and she galloped away with the Court.

"Janet my darling," said Tamlinn, "your amazing courage and love have saved me. Now that I am mortal again, I hope we can marry soon."

"It cannot be too soon for me," said Janet, as she

pushed open the big door of Oakwood Castle. "Being mortal, you will now be hungry," she suggested, "I think we should raid the larder."

When morning lit the windows of Janet's home, it found the two young people sitting on casks in the larder, devouring pies, and hearing the birds of Carterhaugh woods singing their wedding song.

5. The Tailor's Apprentice

Doodie just couldn't eat his breakfast. He was too excited, for he was leaving home that day to go with Mr. Bryden to learn the tailoring trade.

His mother hovered about him, saying, "Now, you'll be a good laddie, mind your manners, keep your nails clean, and learn what Mr. Bryden has to teach you." She added with satisfaction, "You'll get good food at the farms you visit with him, and I hope that will fatten you a bit." No wonder she said that, for poor thin Doodie was known to his companions as 'skinnymalink'.

It was not long before they heard the sound of horses' hoofs on the cobblestones of the village High Street, and looking outside, saw the tailor mounted on his grey mare, his saddlebags bulging with the tools of his craft, and beside him the pack pony which Doodie was to ride. It looked as if there would scarcely be room on the creature which was already burdened with rolls of cloth; a good job perhaps, that its rider was so light.

How proud he felt sitting on the pony in his best suit, annoyed that his mother hindered them, saying, "You'll be careful of him, Mr. Bryden, he's my only son."

The tailor nodded his head, he was in a hurry to be off and didn't notice the mother's tears as they rode down the village street, where heads peeped from behind window curtains and women remarked, "Aye, that's the widow's son, going for to learn a trade."

The tailors spent the summer months visiting the farms in the countryside to make suits or alter clothes, and Doodie and his master were on their way to visit one called Delorain. Doodie looked about him as they travelled for miles into the hills to the lonely house. Usually tailors were very welcome, as they carried news from farm to farm, but the mistress of Delorain who met them at the door scowled and spoke in a crabbit voice; indeed, some people thought she was a witch.

"Ye're late," she said, "ye'll no' want breakfast." But the travellers had started early and wanted a bite before beginning work.

"Ye'll not grudge us a sup of porridge, wife," said the tailor, as he led the horses to the shed and removed the gear. "Have ye much work for us?"

"A suit to the good man and to make-down a coat of his for me," she replied gruffly as she slammed two bowls of porridge before them and two bowls of creamy milk.

"Good fare, wife," said the tailor when his bowl was empty, "but a sup more milk would be welcome."

"You're greedy," she grumbled as she sauchled[1] to the dairy, leaving the door open, which allowed the inquisitive Doodie to step through behind her unseen. He was surprised that, instead of seeing basins of milk, he saw the mistress turn on a spigot[2] set in the wall, from which the milk

---

[1] shuffled   [2] tap

came pouring, and he nipped back to his place at the table without being seen.

When they had finished, the workers cleared the big table and the tailor spread out his woollen cloth and started to cut out the suit, while he handed the scissors and an old coat of the farmer's to Doodie and told him to unpick the seams. The farm-wife went off to collect the hens' eggs. But Doodie was too excited with his new experience to sit still, and went to the window where he saw a pig.

"A grumphie!" he cried, "see? It's a grumphie!"

"I ken it's a grumphie. Sit doon, ye gomeril, and work." Just as Doodie was taking up the scissors again, a hen strayed into the kitchen.

"It's a hen!" cried Doodie, "see? It's a hen!"

"Sure it's a hen, ye daft loon. Get back to your work." Doodie cut a few more stiches when there was a noise from a cupboard, and he went to see.

"It's kittlins," he called, "see? It's kittlins!"

"Aye, I see it's kittlins, and if you don't get back to your work I'll send ye back to your mither." This threat was enough to keep the lad pick-picking away at the old coat.

Presently the master announced: "Yon porridge must have had an awful lot of salt in it. I've a powerful thirst. The mean old curmudgeon doesna keep ale, but I could do with another drink of milk. Do you think you could get me a sup of milk, Doodie?"

"I ken where to get it," said Doodie proudly, and picking up a jug, went into the dairy. He held the jug under the spigot and turned it on, and to his pride and delight, the milk poured into it.

"Aye. I ken how to get milk," he boasted. The jug was full and he turned off the tap, but that did not stop the milk flowing. It spilled over the jug, on to a shelf, off the shelf on to the floor. Very alarmed, Doodie turned the spigot first this way and then that, but the milk kept flowing.

"You asked for milk," he shouted to his master, "aweel, ye've got it!" Mr. Bryden put his head round the door.

"Turn that spigot off, you ediot!" he shouted.

"*You* turn it off," said the frightened lad. The tailor also turned the tap this way and that, and still the milk poured out, till the floor was inches deep in creamy milk.

"See what you've done, you fool!" shouted the master splashing about, and just then the housewife returned from the barn with her apron full of new-laid eggs.

"Ye meddlesome fools!" she cried, letting go her hold of the apron so that all the eggs fell to the floor, but most of them floated around in the milk. "Do you ken what ye've done?" she shrieked. "That's the collected milk from all the cows in the district — and when the girls go in the evening to milk their cows, not a drop will they get. They may sing to the cows, and pull at the teats, but not a drop will they get, for you have spilled it all. Many awkward questions will be asked and it's all your fault." The milk was now up to their ankles and splashing about everywhere.

The frightened tailor and his small helper hurried back to work, but in his excitement Mr. Bryden cut two left sleeves and only one trouser leg, and Doodie's hands were trembling so that he could not find the stitches.

"Is she a witch?" he asked. He got no reply, but his master grabbed the scissors, bundled up the spoiled material and headed for the horses. The farmer's wife went after them.

"If you tell *anyone* what you saw," she said, glowering at them like a wild animal, "if you do, I'll put such a thirst on you for ever that the waters of three lochs would not quench it. Do you hear?"

Aye, they heard, and could not ride away quickly enough.

"Certainly the wife of Delorain is a witch," said Mr. Bryden.

6. The Cauldron

Old Mairi and Angus lived very happily in their croft cottage away in the hills. They had two dogs, a cow, and hens, so they did not want for butter, milk, cheese and eggs, but you would wonder how they got meat. The town was too far away for a butcher, and Angus was too old to shoot deer. Yet every day they had meat and bones for the dogs, and how they got it was a secret. When Mairi would be sweeping the room in the morning, and the big black pot would be standing empty by the fire, a pretty faerie-woman would appear and take hold of the cauldron. Then Mairi would stop whatever she was doing and say:

> Dleasaidh gobha gual
> Gu idruinn guar a bhruich
> Dleasaidh coire cunimh
> 'S chur slán teach

which is Gaelic and means:

> A smith is entitled to his coals
> In order cold iron to heat
> A cauldron's entitled to the bones
> And to be sent home whole,

and then the faerie would fly away with the cauldron. In the evening, the faerie would bring the cauldron back, full of meat and bones.

One day, before the faerie had arrived, Mairi was going to the village to sell some of their eggs. She would be away all day, so she said to Angus, "Now Angus, you will remember when the faerie comes to say to her exactly what I say."

"Of course, of course," said Angus.

"You won't forget, will you?"

"No, no, I won't forget."

"You had best get on with mending the roof," she said, "the hens have been tearing at the thatch again."

"I will, I will," agreed Angus. So away went Mairi for the day, and Angus got the ladder and some newly-cut heather to mend the roof. It was a job he liked, and he was sitting up there working away and whistling a tune to himself, when he saw the faerie coming. She was gliding through the air with a green light all about her, and Angus was afraid. He came down the ladder in a great hurry, ran indoors and slammed the door shut.

"Let me in," said the faerie, but Angus was more frightened than ever and he put his hands over his face. The faerie was angry, and because he would not open the door, she came down the chimney. That is when he should have said:

> A smith is entitled to his coals
> In order cold iron to heat
> A cauldron's entitled to the bones
> And to be sent home whole,

but he was so scared, he forgot altogether. The faerie grabbed the great pot and disappeared back up the chimney.

It was late evening when Mairi returned. She was tired and hungry, and looked forward to a bowl of soup made from the bones in the cauldron.

"I see you have not done much to the roof, Angus," she said, and then she noticed that the big black pot was not over the fire.

"Where's the cauldron?" she shouted. "Angus, where's the cauldron?"

"Ah well," said her husband unhappily, "the faerie woman took it."

"And did you say what I always say?"

"I — I forgot," stammered Angus.

"You good-for-nothing fool! Where will we get meat now?"

"I'm sorry, but don't make such a fuss, wife. She will come back." But she didn't come back, and they were eating eggs boiled, eggs scrambled, eggs fried, eggs poached every day, and no meat.

Till at last Mairi said: "I'm going to get the cauldron back."

"Don't interfere with the faerie folk," warned Angus, "it is dangerous to do so," but Mairi would not be put off, and though it was getting dark, she set off for the faerie hillock.

The piece of rock that was the door in the faerie-hill was set aside, so she could enter, and inside she saw the cauldron over a fire, and two old men sitting beside it, fast asleep. Mairi tiptoed in and grabbed the great pot which was full of meat and bones. She was almost out with it, but accidentally knocked it against the door, and it let out a screech which wakened the two men.

One of them started at once to chase her, but he was old and could not catch her, so he shouted to the other one: "Let out the dogs!" and there leapt out of the hillock two enormous green hounds, with blazing red eyes. Mairi could not run very fast because the cauldron was so heavy with the meat in it and all, and the heather caught at her feet. The dogs were catching up on her, indeed they were almost at her heels. In a panic, she threw a bone behind, and the two ferocious hounds stopped to pick it up. That let Mairi get a bit nearer home, but she was so out of breath and so tired she thought she could not move another inch. She ran a little way, and then threw out another bone. The hounds started to quarrel over this, and she managed to dash through the open door of the cottage. She was trembling like a jelly as she banged the door shut, just as their own two dogs rushed out barking and the hounds ran away.

Angus and Mairi had meat that day, and next morning they waited and waited, but the faerie wife never came again, and after that Angus had to set rabbit snares if they wanted any meat.

7. Blue-Caps

Fionag was born and brought up on the Little Island, but she had longed for the town and had taken a job as a maid to a family in the town. At first, she found the bright lights and busy streets great fun, but after a while she became tired of the noise and the dust, and longed to go back to her Little Island.

Though her parents were dead, and there was hardly anyone left there, she wanted to see the big sky full of stars at night, and hear the seagulls quarrelling and the tide lap-lapping against the rocks.

"You'll never get married there," people warned her, but Fionag returned to the Island and found a young fisherman, Duncan. He seemed so much sturdier and more active than the town lads, and soon they fell in love and were married. They lived simply and happily for years in the little cottage, but after a while, Fionag began to

35

want some of the things she had possessed in the town.

"It would be so nice," she thought, "to go into shops and buy nice things like cups and spoons and bright-coloured rugs."

One evening, Duncan was searching for the cows which had strayed over the hill, when he heard a noise like people chattering, and when he pushed through the bracken to see who it could possibly be, there was the sound of scampering feet, though no one else now lived on the Island. He saw no one, but what he *did* see was three beautiful plates, three gold goblets and three silver spoons lying on the patch of grass.

"How I wish I could take them to Fionag," he thought. But he was an honest man, and he left them lying there, but on returning home he told her about his amazing discovery.

"Go later this evening," she said, "we must find out to whom such lovely things belong." So Duncan went at night and hid in the bracken to watch. For a while nothing happened, so he picked up the lovely things to examine them, wishing again that he could take them home to Fionag, then he put them down and waited in his hiding-place. He heard a rustle in the bracken and three little men, each wearing a blue cap, went forward to the things.

"Someone has touched this plate," said one little man.

"Someone has touched this goblet," said another.

"Someone has touched the spoons," said another.

"We cannot use them now that he has handled them," they all said together.

"Never mind," said one, "there are plenty more where those came from." Then they put on their little blue caps and cried, "Away to London to the King's house," and they all rose in the air like thistledown in the wind and were gone!

Duncan picked up the plates, the goblets and the spoons,

and went home. When Fionag heard her husband coming, she ran to the door.

"Oh Duncan! How lovely! I never saw anything so beautiful, even in town." They ate their oatcakes and cheese from the plates, their porridge with the silver spoons, and drank their milk from the golden goblets.

"You will be content now, my love," said Duncan, seeing her happiness reflected on her face.

"Perhaps if we give them something in return, they will bring more," said his wife. "My mirror is cracked, and my comb has lost some teeth, but put them where you found the beautiful things and we will see what happens."

So Duncan put the mirror and comb in the same spot next morning, and in the evening went to see what had happened, and there in the place of Fionag's old things, lay a beautiful silver mirror and silver comb. He was just in time to see the three little men don their blue caps and cry, "Away to London to the King's house" and disappear into the sky.

"You will be content now," said Duncan to his wife, seeing her happy smile as she looked into the mirror while she combed her hair.

"Well, indeed these are beautiful," Fionag said, "but take that old rag rug from the door to them and let's see what happens." Duncan did so, and that evening brought back the most exquisite rug.

"*Now* my love, you will be content, you never saw such a rug as that."

"Indeed I am pleased, but Duncan, my old clothes look silly beside it," and she handed him her old ragged, faded brown dress to take to the wee men. Duncan put the dress in the special place and went back that night. The three men were just laying out a gorgeous silken dress of yellow velvet, and then, "Away to London to the King's house" and they were off.

Duncan was so proud to see his wife in such a dress,

she looked like a princess.

"You cannot want more than that," he said, "you must be content *now*."

"But Duncan," said Fionag, "look at my awful old bauchles[1] peeping out from under this lovely gown, I must have slippers fit to wear with it." So Duncan put her old shoes in the green place, and next night brought back a pair of lovely golden slippers. Such clothes were no use for working on the croft, but at night Fionag would dress up and they would sit with their feet on the warm rug and eat and drink from the lovely vessels.

I must find out where Duncan goes, thought Fionag, so one night she followed him without being seen. The next evening Duncan came in from work to find that she had taken their two chairs away.

"What are we going to sit on?" he grumbled.

"We will sit on the floor," said his wife. Next day, there were two important-looking chairs where the little men had left them. The day after, Duncan came in tired, for he had worked late at the hay.

"I'll go early to bed," he said, and then exclaimed "Where's the bed? — no bed? Where are we to sleep?"

"On the floor," said his wife.

Because they were most uncomfortable on the hard floor, Duncan was out early in the morning and found the little men struggling with a great four-poster bed, feather mattress, soft blankets, velvet curtains and all. They laughed as they put on their blue caps and shouted, "Away to London and the King's house."

Duncan had to go and get Fionag to help with such a heavy piece of furniture, and when they had it set up it was so big that the cottage door could hardly be opened or shut, and they were terribly tired, but they slept in the luxurious bed as if on a cloud.

"My love, there simply cannot be anything more that

[1] shoes

38

you want. You *must* be content *now*," said Duncan. But Fionag thought of new pots and pans, of jugs and lamps, and all these gradually appeared in the cottage till it was more like a palace than a crofter's cottage.

There was only one thing that Duncan wanted, and that was some wine, for he thought it a shame to drink milk out of the gold goblets. So he set an old empty ale bottle on the green patch, and went that night hopefully for the only thing he had asked for himself. The three little men were there with a great supply of wine, and were enjoying drinking and singing. Duncan thought it was a pity not to join them, and came out of his usual hiding-place to do so. This so frightened the little men that they rushed away, but one of them accidentally dropped his blue cap.

Duncan snatched it up and put it on his own head. "Away to London and the King's house," he said, and was immediately up in the air, floating over the cottage, over the glen, over the sea, buffeted about as if in a whirlwind. Then all was suddenly silent and dark and he found himself in a wine cellar. The door opened and a soldier stood before him.

"Ha ha! We've caught the thief at last," he said. But he spoke a language that Duncan did not understand, and took him before a judge, who asked him questions that Duncan could not answer because he could only understand the Gaelic.

"This man," said the judge, "has stolen chairs and goblets and rugs and wine from the King's palace. He is a thief and must die. I order that he be hanged tomorrow."

Poor Duncan. He could not explain, but he saw the gallows being made ready and knew that he was to die. He was led to the scaffold and the rope was being made ready, when he suddenly remembered the little blue cap in his pocket. He bashed it on his head and shouted, "Away to the Island," and in what seemed a minute, he was floating down on the edge of the tide on the Island. He ran to the cottage, and opening the door, saw Fionag sitting by the fire weeping.

"I would rather have *nothing*, nothing at all," she sobbed, "if only I could have my dear Duncan again. Just to have him, I would be completely content for ever."

Just as she said this, all the beautiful new things they had got from the little men in the blue caps vanished; there were the old chairs by the fire, the old mended rug, the thick china cups on the dresser and no velvet gown or golden slippers to be seen.

Then she saw Duncan.

"Oh dear!" he exclaimed. "Look what's happened."

"I don't care," said Fionag, hugging him. "I would rather have you than all the loveliest things in the world."

your luck-your luck

8. The Simple Lad

There were three young lads who were friends and lived together. Hector was the youngest and was called the Simple Lad, because he often had tricks played on him, but he worked harder than the other two and soon possessed four cows, while the other two, called Rory and Para, only had two each.

"Why have we only two cows and he has four?" they asked each other, and they felt so angry about it that they went at night and killed Hector's cows, and then said to him, "It is too bad that robbers have killed your cattle."

Instead of wasting time getting angry (though he knew fine that the other two had killed his cows) Hector said: "Well, dead is dead, I can't make my cattle come alive again, so I must do the best I can," and he skinned the animals and salted the meat so that he could eat it when the winter came. He took one of the skins and made four pockets in it, and in each pocket he put a silver coin. Then he folded the skin carefully and carried it on his head to the market.

As he passed through a wood on the way, a starling flew down and pecked at the hide, but Hector quickly put up his hand and caught the bird.

"Ha ha, I was too quick for you," he said. "Such is your luck." He was very surprised when the bird repeated the last two words, "Your luck, your luck," and he took some bread from his pocket to feed the starling. They met a man riding from the market, who saw the skin on Hector's head and the bird in his hand.

"Is that a tame bird?" he asked.

"Yes," said Hector, "and it can tell your fortune. Ask it."

"If I buy you, what can you do for me?" the gentleman asked the starling, and it replied: "Your luck, your luck," and Hector gave it some more food.

"Will you sell that bird?" asked the gentleman. "How much do you want for it?"

"Four gold coins," said Hector.

"That's a lot of money, but I need a bit of luck just now," said the rider, and gave Hector the money and rode away with the bird. When he got home, the gentleman found that a man who owed him money had just paid up.

"This bird has brought me luck," he told his wife. But soon after, he found that the man had paid him in false coins, and the bird never said a word again. "I've been swindled," said the gentleman.

When Hector got to the market, he walked up and down saying: "I want four gold coins for my hide." The people laughed at him.

"It's Simple Hector," they said, "the skin isn't worth more than ten sixpences."

"But," said Hector, "this is not like other skins."

"Well," asked a farmer, "what's different about that hide, that you expect so much money?"

"Come to a quiet place and I'll show you," said Hector. So they went to a quiet place, where Hector spread the skin carefully on the ground, then he cut a big stick and hit the skin hard so that one of the silver coins fell out of the pocket. The farmer was even more surprised when Hector did the same again and another coin fell out. He gaped in amazement. Hector gave him the stick.

"Do it yourself," he said, and the farmer did so.

When the third coin fell out, he said: "I'll give you your price for this hide," and gave Hector four gold coins. So Hector went home, and at the supper table he laid out the four gold coins.

"How did you get them?" asked Para.

"I suppose you stole them," said Rory.

"No. I got that money because someone killed my cows, and I had a skin to sell."

Para and Rory thought: "If *he* can get four gold coins for a skin, so can we," and they killed their own cows, skinned them and set off for the market, where they went about saying: "Hides for eight gold pieces." But the farmer who had bought the hide from Hector was there.

"Here is another swindler," he shouted, "I bought a hide for four gold pieces that was supposed to be able to give me silver coins when I beat it, and I've beaten it till it is in shreds, and I am so tired I can hardly move my arms, and never a coin to be seen." And everyone started to beat Rory and Para so that they went home in a hurry, with their hides unsold and no cows either!

They were so angry with Hector that they took him while he slept and, pushing him into an empty barrel, they closed down the lid, and intended to throw it over a cliff. But the barrel was heavy, the day hot, and they were thirsty, so they went into an Inn for a drink, leaving the barrel outside. A shepherd came by and he was thirsty too, but he had no money.

"If I just had enough to get me a drink," he said, so

Hector started banging on the inside of the barrel and shouting: "Gold and silver, gold and silver, open the barrel for gold and silver." The astonished shepherd prised off the lid, and out came Hector.

"I don't see any gold or silver," said the shepherd, peering into the barrel.

"Oh, you have to get inside to find it. It's at the bottom," said Hector. He took the bonnet and plaid and crook off the shepherd, while the shepherd got into the barrel, and Hector slammed down the lid.

By the time Rory and Para came out of the Inn, Hector had walked away in the shepherd's clothing. The two picked up the barrel and set off for the cliff.

"We'll fling it far out into the sea," said Para.

Then the frightened shepherd banged on the barrel and called out: "Don't do that! It's *me*! It's me!"

"Of course it's you," said the brothers, and they rolled the barrel over the edge of the cliff and went back home. On the way, they found Hector driving a nice flock of sheep. At first, they thought he must be a ghost, for they were sure he must have been killed when the barrel fell into the sea.

"Where did you get those sheep?" they asked him.

"I got the sheep," said Hector, "from the Otherworld below the sea. You have only to ask for them, for the people there have more sheep than they need."

"How do you get there?" asked Para greedily.

"You go as I went, in the barrel." So the two brothers got barrels and Hector closed the lids and pushed them over the cliff. To his surprise, the barrels floated, but the tide took them out to sea, where they were picked up by a pirate ship.

"What are you doing in such a place?" the Captain of the ship asked them.

"We were looking for sheep," said Para.

"Looking for sheep in the middle of the sea! You're

crazy mad," said the Captain, and he took them to a foreign land and sold them as slaves to the natives.

Hector by this time was very rich, and so from calling him the Simple Lad, people said: "He's no sae daft after all."

9. Muckle Mouthed Meg

Meg, daughter of Sir Gideon of Elibank, was looking in the mirror. Poor Meg, it made her so unhappy. She had lovely curly brown hair, a rather impudent little nose, and a very big mouth, and she could almost cry when people called her 'Muckle Mouthed Meg'. Her two sisters were good-looking, but even they were not yet married, so what chance had Meg?

Over the hill lived Willie Scott and his mother. Willie was rather a wild young man, but who could blame him? For what was there for a lively lad to do except raid other folk's cattle?

"Come on!" he said to old Simon, a favourite serving-man. "Let's lift some of the Elibank cattle. He has a huge herd." So on a moonlight night, Willie and Simon mounted their strong Border horses and rode for Sir Gideon of Elibank's estate.

Sir Gideon's cattle were grazing a long way from the castle, so it was easy enough, going slowly, to herd them back towards the Scotts' home of Harden. But it was a long way, the beasts got tired and Willie got hungry, so halfway home they stopped, and when the cattle were settled down, they went to gather firewood to make a fire for a meal. It was while they were separated on this ploy, that they were horrified to hear the sound of barking hounds, and the cry of "Elibank! Elibank!" and before they could get to their weapons, they were struggling and outnumbered. Willie fought like a mad thing, but both he and Simon were taken prisoner, and with both hands and feet tied, they were thrown over their horses' backs and taken triumphantly to Elibank Castle.

Elibank himself was delighted. There had been a feud between the two families for years, and here was Willie Scott, the only son of his enemy, delivered into his hands.

"I'll hang him the morn," Sir Gideon shouted with glee. "Aye, I'll hang him the morn."

"That would be a daft-like thing to do," said his wife. "You've got a bonny lad of property in the house and you've three unmarried daughters. We need a wedding, not a hanging. Marry him to Meg."

"He'd never marry Meg! our muckle mouthed lass — never!"

"Aye, he would so, if you told him it would be the girl or the gallows for him."

"That's a grand idea!" Elibank roared with laughter.

Willie and Simon were shut up in a room so small that it was more like a cupboard, and old Simon was in tears thinking of his wife and children, when Sir Gideon suddenly flung open the door.

"I'll give ye a chance, Willie," he said grinning. "If ye'll marry my daughter Meg, ye'll no need to hang."

"Marry Muckle Mouthed Meg! Never! I will *not*!" shouted Willie.

"Oh Master, please," pleaded Simon. "It's better to be wed and alive than to be hanging dead from a tree." But Willie would not listen.

"I'd sooner be hanged," he said.

"Well, it's hanged you'll be," said Sir Gideon, banging the door shut; then he opened it again to say, "I'll no hang the old man."

"If you hang Master Willie, I'll hang too," said Simon, but Willie persuaded him that he would still be needed at Harden. Then Willie went to the wee window to look out on what he knew would be his last sunset.

Elibank told his wife and daughters, "Willie would rather be hanged than marry our Meg." But Meg had her own ideas. She dressed as a serving-maid and took the prisoners their supper.

"I'm terribly sorry about you," she said to Willie. "I would do *anything* to save you. Is there anything I can do to help? Would you like me to take a message to your poor mother? She must be worrying terribly."

"Thank you," said Willie, "that is a kind thought. Get me paper and pen and I'll write it now. But it will not be very safe for a young lass to go all that distance in the black of night."

"I am not afraid," said Meg, "who would interfere with a servant?" So Willie wrote his letter, and Meg set off in the darkness, and arriving safe, had the message delivered to Mistress Scott who was very grateful.

"Bring the servant to me," she ordered, and then told Meg, "He writes that he could be saved if he would marry Muckle Mouthed Meg, but — oh dear! He says he would rather be hanged! Tell him from me that he *must* marry her. He *must*. What sort of a lass is this girl Meg?" she asked the servant.

"Oh, she's no bonny — something like myself, but she's kind, and I think she loves your Willie." Meg took the mother's message back to the prisoner.

48

"Marry Muckle Mouthed Meg! I will *not*!" said Willie, and Meg burst into tears.

Next morning, Willie was led out to the hanging tree, and the noose was put round his neck. There was a big crowd to watch, and Meg was there, wearing a hood that hid her face. Sir Gideon was just going to raise his hand as a signal for the rope to be pulled, when Meg ran up to him and whispered, "Wait, Father. Ask him if he would wed the serving girl who took the message to his mother." Rather astonished, for her father had known nothing of Meg's trick, he went up to the doomed young man and asked, "Would you marry the servant lass who took a message to your mother?"

"Well," said Willie, thinking hard and remembering Meg's brave journey and her tears, "she was no bonny, but she was a brave and kindly lass. A man could do worse, yes, I'd marry her."

Meg came forward shyly, pushing back her hood, and as she unbound his hands, he put his arms round her.

"Ye're a kind-hearted brave one," he said. "I'll be proud to marry you." So there was a wedding instead of a hanging, with dancing and feasting.

"We're eating the Elibank cattle after all!" laughed Simon as he gobbled the roast beef. Willie and Meg were a very happy married couple, and from them was descended the great author, Sir Walter Scott.

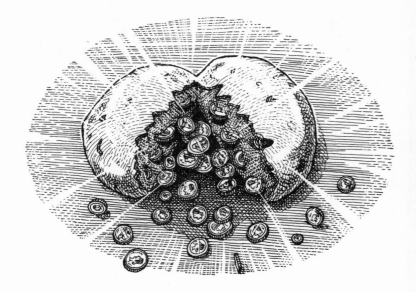

10. The Bannock of Tollishill

Pretty Maggie Leystone married Thomas Hardie and they were very happy in their house of Tollishill, high among the Border hills where he kept his sheep. The first winter together was very severe, but Thomas managed to raise just enough sheep to pay the rent to their landlord, the Earl of Lauderdale. But the second winter was cruel, snowdrifts and blizzards spoilt the lambing and there was no money for rent. The landlord, knowing how hard it had been, said he would wait till next year for the rent, but then both years must be paid.

However the next winter was worse than ever, sheep were buried under the snow, lambs were lost, there was no early pasture, and so again there was no money for the rent. The Earl sent word that either the rent would be paid or they would be turned out of the house. Where could they go? They could not live in that bleak situation without shelter, and they had no money to live on. Thomas could only sit by the small fire gazing miserably at his young wife and wondering what would become of them — and Maggie wept because she did not know what to do, and could not help. Then she had an idea.

"I will go myself to the landlord, Tom, surely he will listen and give us another chance?"

"Not he," said Tom, "don't you lower yourself, he will only sneer."

But Maggie thought it worth the chance, and though the snow was thick on the hills, and every now and again a blizzard would blow, she wrapped herself in her biggest plaid and set off the eight and a half miles to Thirlestane Castle to see the Earl. The cold wind whistled shrilly and the flying snow hit her face like bullets, she fell into a snowdrift and scrambled out again only to find that she had lost her way, but the shape of a familiar hill gave her direction again, and she plodded on, having to lift her feet high at each step on the snow-blanketed moors.

She was so tired when she got to the Castle that she had to sit on the steps for a while before she could rise to ring the great bell. The noise of it clanged like an alarm and a surly-looking servant opened the door and then slammed it in her face before she could speak. Maggie rang again, but there was no answer. She felt angry. Had she come all this way in vain? She took up a stone and banged on the door with it. The same man opened it.

"Go away," he said, but just at that moment the Earl was crossing the entrance and caught sight of the girl standing on the doorstep — he liked a pretty face, and told the servant to let her in.

"Bring her to the library," he said. The servant was annoyed at such a visitor but had to do as he was bid.

"What is it you want?" the Earl asked gruffly.

"Sir, I am from Tollishill, and — and —" She was nearly crying as the warmth of the house thawed her half-frozen

51

fingers and feet. "It has been a bad winter, the snow lasting so late, and we have lost sheep and the lambing —"

The Earl interrupted her angrily. "What a lot of nonsense," he bellowed. "I must have my rents, it's ridiculous to blame the late snow."

Maggie could not prevent her tears. "It will be better next year," she said, "and then we will be able to pay all we owe you."

The Earl smiled. "How do you know it will not be late snow again next year?" he asked.

Maggie could only repeat, "Please, please."

"Well," said the Earl with a laugh, "I will make a bargain with you. As you blame your troubles on the late snow, if you can bring me a snowball in the month of June, I will forget about the rent." How impossible, what a cruel thing to say! But he did send Maggie to the kitchen to be given a good meal before she struggled back across the hills.

It was almost dark before she got back, and Tom was so worried that he had lit a lantern and was going to go in search of her, when she came in and flung herself into his arms, telling him of the Earl's bargain.

"How cruel to make such a mock of you! Snow in June, indeed! Fine he knows that's impossible." Thomas gently took off her sodden shoes and stockings, sat her by the fire and gave her some hot soup to drink. After that Maggie felt more cheerful and as she was not one to give in easily, she thought how she might yet make the Earl keep his bargain.

So next day, she went secretly from the house with a basket which she filled with snow. This she took to a small cave on the side of a hill on which the sun never shone. She pressed the snow into a tight ball, covered it with wet moss, and set it at the back of the cave. She did not tell her husband.

On the first day in June, she again went secretly to the

cave. It was almost impossible after all those weeks of warm spring weather that the snowball should still be there. "I shall only find a puddle of water," she thought. But she was wrong, for the snowball was still there, and she shivered with excitement as she wound it in a damp cloth and placed it in the basket. She did not wait to return home. She could not help it if Tom was worried by her absence. She must run as fast as she could that eight and a half miles to Thirlestane Castle. Suppose the Earl should be away! Or even if the snowball had not entirely melted, could she really believe he would keep his promise? She rang the bell, and explained that she must see the Earl in a hurry.

"Please, I must see him just at once," she said with an alarmed look at the basket. The Earl was amazed and amused when his tenant stood in front of him and drew the cloth aside to hand him a small, dripping snowball.

"A snowball in June," said Maggie, "you remember you promised to forget the rent if I brought you a snowball in June."

"Well, you are a determined lassie," said the Earl. "Yes, my dear, I'll keep my promise and never mind about the rent this year." He offered her food but Maggie was in too much of a hurry to give Tom her good news, and dashed back over the moors as if she had wings on her feet.

They hugged each other in their joy and started to plan what would help the farm in future.

The next year was a prosperous one. Tom was able to buy more sheep and so have more lambs for sale, so it was easy to pay the rent.

But if it was a fortunate time for the Hardies, it was not so for the Earl. He was in sore trouble and had been taken prisoner when fighting the intruder Cromwell, and sent to the Tower of London. Most of the Earl's tenants were delighted that in his absence they would not need to pay rent to him, but the Hardies, remembering how he had kept his promise, did not spend the rent money, but put it aside every year till it grew to be a large sum.

"But what use is it to the Earl?" asked Tom.

"It would be useful to bribe his prison warders and he could escape to France," Maggie said.

"But we can't get it to him," objected Tom.

"We could take it to him," announced his wife.

"What! Go to London? You're daft! Even if I could walk all that way, with all that wealth on me, I would be robbed before I was two miles over the Border!"

"I'll come with you," said Maggie.

"No you won't! A bag of gold and a bonny lass also would be a worse danger than ever," objected Tom. But Maggie put on a pair of his trousers and shoved her hair under a Scots bonnet and looked a lively lad. Before they set off, she baked a big round bannock of barley meal. It was so thick that she had been able to hide the gold sovereigns of the rent in it before she baked it. "Who would want to steal a bannock?" she laughed.

So they set off, trudging for days and weary days, the gold safe in the bannock even when they had to sleep under hedges.

When they were near London they met General Monk who was travelling to Scotland; he was known as 'Kind Geordie' and he was interested in the two travellers, especially as he saw through Maggie's disguise. Her shoes had worn through so she had discarded them, and Geordie was sure he had never seen so pretty a pair of feet on a laddie. Being found out, they told him of their plan and how they wanted to get the money to the Earl of Lauderdale. The General so admired the honesty and loyalty of the pair that he even said he would see if he could use his influence to help the escape of the prisoner, and wished them good luck.

Maggie was almost too weary to put one foot before another by the time they reached the Tower, and the warders and guards would not let them go to the Earl's prison cell. Then Maggie changed her clothes to her own which she had brought in a bundle, and sat on the wall and sang to the guards. They were glad to listen, and though she sang Scots songs which they could not understand, they agreed that 'the girl had a sweet voice' and encouraged her to continue.

"Please may I sing outside the prisoner's window?" she asked. They thought there could be no harm in this, for the window was high up, so Maggie stood below it and sang the tune and song of Lauder Haughs. The homesick Earl was surprised and delighted and went to the window at once to see who could be singing such a song. He begged the warders to let the singer in to see him.

"What harm can a young girl like that do?" they thought, "she is obviously just a servant." So Maggie stood before her landlord and his eye brightened at the sight of her.

"Maggie from Tollishill!" he said. "And what are you doing in London? Have you come to offer me another snowball?"

"No my lord," and she joined in his laughter. "I've brought you a bannock of barley meal."

"What a big bannock, my dear! But I doubt it will be pretty stale by now."

"Taste it, my lord."

"I'll break my teeth on it," he objected.

"Then break it with your hands." The prisoner took it in his hands and broke off a piece, showing some of the golden coins. He was so surprised that at first he could not speak.

"It is your own," said Maggie, "for it is the rents for the years you have been away. We have not forgotten you kept your promise over the snowball." The Earl was so grateful that he kissed her hand.

"You are a wonderful, honest, loyal couple," he said.

"I will not forget. I guess no bigger or better bannock was ever made at Tollishill."

He insisted that she keep enough money for them to travel home by coach and after they had returned they were delighted to hear that the Earl had escaped to France and might soon be returning to Scotland.

So he did, and was given a high position, but one of the first things he did was to pay a visit to Tollishill accompanied by many rich nobles. Maggie and her husband went to the door to meet them, surprised at such great company, and the Earl dismounted and thanked them for their loyalty, and at the same time he put round Maggie's waist the most beautiful silver belt, which is preserved today in the Museum of Antiquities in Edinburgh.

11. Findlay and the Giants

Findlay lived with his sister Minla, and went hunting every day. Before he set out he would say, "Do not open the north window nor let the fire out," for the north window let in the cold wind and he needed a fire to warm him when he returned.

She would always reply, "I will neither shut nor open any window nor let the fire out." Minla was a bad sister, and as soon as her brother was out of sight she would open the north window and stamp out the fire.

One day Findlay was returning home very tired when he saw a small house that he had never noticed before. He wondered who lived there and knocked on the door. There was no reply so he went in and saw an old woman sitting by the fire.

"Sit down, Findlay," she said. "I know all about you and your bad sister. She is hoping that you will be killed this very day."

57

"I do not believe she is so bad as that," said Findlay.

"She is indeed so. She has made a couch for you before the fire in your room, and under it a giant is hidden waiting to kill you." Findlay went home and was met by Minla.

"You will be tired, brother," she said smiling, "I have made a nice couch for you to rest."

Findlay pretended that he knew nothing about the hidden giant. He always washed his feet when he came home from hunting, and for this he required a pot of boiling water, but instead of putting it on the floor he deliberately set it on the couch. Then he had his dinner, and having eaten the meat he threw the bones on to the couch for the hunting dogs. The great hounds scrambled over the couch quarrelling and snapping at each other till they had the pot of boiling water overturned. Up jumped the scalded giant, and ran out of the house screaming, taking Minla with him. Findlay was pleased, but he knew that there were more giants where that one came from, and that they would certainly come to kill him.

Indeed he was right, for in a cave were the mother and father giant and a younger brother. When they saw the blisters on the one who had gone to kill Findlay, they were very angry.

"It is I who will go and kill Findlay," said the father giant.

"Nay, it is I who will go and kill Findlay," said the mother giant.

"It is I who will go and kill Findlay," said the younger brother, and strode out of the cave, making the earth shake with his big strides and a noise like thunder with his breathing. "Hoy, Ha, Ho, let me in!" he shouted.

Findlay had no intention of doing any such thing, but the young giant bashed the door in. Findlay was behind that door with his bow and arrow, and shot the giant in the arm. The young giant did not seem to mind and rushed at Findlay, but the two great hounds attacked him and killed him. Findlay cut off the giant's head and took it to the old woman who had warned him about the couch.

"Good, good. 'Tis the hero you are," she said. But Findlay was honest and told her that he could never have beaten the giant without the help of the dogs.

When he returned home that night, the father giant was just arriving and the size and noise of him nearly made the roof fall in.

"Hoy, Ha, Ho!" bellowed the giant. Findlay shot three arrows into him, but again it was the dogs that helped, and Findlay was able to cut off the giant's head and take it to his friend, the old lady.

"Good, good. 'Tis the hero you are, but this night the old hag mother giant will come. Beware, for she will look like an ordinary woman and will seem to be harmless, but she intends to kill you."

It was a black and silent night when a knock came at the door and an old woman asked, "May it please you that I come in?"

"Come in," said Findlay, for she seemed a gentle kind of person. She sat to the fire and he noticed that she had fangs instead of teeth.

"Tie up your dogs, please," she said, for they were sniffing round and growling.

"They will not harm you so long as you sit still," said Findlay. "Anyway, I haven't any rope with which to tie them."

"Take these," said the hag, pulling three hairs from her head, "they are so strong they would hold a ship." He made the dogs lie down in a dark corner, but he did not tie them and he put the three hairs into his pocket. When he sat down again opposite the old woman, he thought she had grown larger.

"You are growing bigger," he said.

"No no, it is just that I am cold." But she grew bigger still.

"You *are* growing bigger," Findlay said.

"No, no, it is only the firelight makes me seem so."

"You *are*! You *are*!" he shouted as her head touched the ceiling.

"Well, so I am," she said, and sprang at Findlay. He did not have his bow and arrows beside him and he and the giant hag wrestled on the floor. She had him down. He had her down. She was the stronger and grasped his throat so that no breath was in him, but he used the three hairs to tie her hands and so she was beaten.

"Let me go," she pleaded.

"If I let you go, what can you give me?"

"In the cave I have a box of gold and silver."

"Never mind that," said Findlay.

"I have most beautiful brooches and jewels."

"Never mind those," said Findlay.

"I have a golden sword."

"Never mind that."

"I have a wand that will turn a stone into a warrior, and if you put the golden sword into his hand, no man will be able to best him in a battle."

"Never mind that," said Findlay.

"I have another wand that will turn the warrior back into a stone."

"Never mind that."

"Alas! I have no other thing except my son," and at that moment she broke her bonds and sprang at Findlay and if the two great hounds had not pounced on her, Findlay would have been lying dead. But he cut off her head to take to his friend, the old woman. Her fangs were so huge and so heavy that he could hardly get to the cottage.

"Good, good. 'Tis the hero you are, and now we will go to get the treasure in the cave."

"Not so easy," warned Findlay, "for there is still my old enemy the brother giant in the cave."

"I will bring my magic wand," she said, "and my foster

60

daughter, Geve, will help us." Findlay saw that the foster daughter was very beautiful.

When they neared the cave they could hear the giant snoring, and it sounded like a den of angry lions.

"Let us gather heather," said the foster daughter. They did so, and piling it up at the mouth of the cave, they set fire to it. Soon they heard the brother giant spluttering and coughing with the smoke and knew he would want to escape from it.

"I will shoot him," said Findlay, wanting to show the foster daughter Geve that he was not afraid.

"No," said the old woman, "arrows will not kill him."

"I will send the dogs in to destroy him."

"No, they will choke with the smoke."

"What then?" said Findlay, disappointed.

"I will try to hit him with my magic wand, but if I miss, he will surely kill me."

The giant crawled groaning to the mouth of the cave, was hit by the magic wand and that was the end of him. He was so big that his thumb was larger than Findlay's arm, and they had to scramble over his body. In the back of the cave they found Minla dead from the smoke.

"A bad one, that," said the old woman.

"How could she be unkind to such a wonderful brother?" said Geve. They looked around for the treasure. There it was indeed. Gold and silver, brooches and necklaces, coins and bracelets and the golden sword. The foster daughter found the two magic wands that the old hag had mentioned.

"See if they really are magic," she said. Findlay took one and struck a stone which turned immediately into a tall warrior. He put the golden sword into the warrior's hand, and so terribly fierce did he look that Findlay was afraid and hurriedly struck him with the other wand, which turned him back to stone. They took the treasure back to the cottage, where Geve put on the jewels.

"What should I do next?" Findlay asked the old woman, wanting to show Geve what he could do.

"You will go to the King and tell him that the giants are slain, but you must promise not to go into the King's palace."

Findlay sent the king a message that the giants were all killed, and was invited to the palace, but he would not go. The King and Queen even came to his door to invite him, but Findlay had promised and he would not go. Geve was glad, for she was in love with Findlay and, like her foster mother, she was afraid the King would offer his daughter in marriage to the hero who had killed the giants.

So Findlay came home and married Geve, but not before he had shown the King the work of the magic wands.

After many years the old woman died and so did Geve. Findlay was left alone and thought he would offer to serve the King. When he arrived at the palace, the King had forgotten him, but his daughter said, "I am sure he is the man who turned a stone into a warrior."

"I do not recognise him," said the King, "but if he is, he is also the hero who killed the giants and I will give him half my kingdom, and your hand in marriage."

So Findlay married the Princess and when her father died, became King himself.

12. The Gaberlunzie Man

The farmer was giving a great feast, because it was harvest time, and the corn was all safe in stacks. The big barn had tables in it that were loaded with food. All the farm hands in the district were gathered at this farm called Cairn-kebbie to have fun, and the farmer, William Hume, and his wife were particularly proud of their daughter, Lily.

Everyone was dressed in their best holiday clothes, but Lily, in her long green skirt, which she had tucked up to join in the dances that followed the supper, was the bonniest of them all. Young Bill Kerr certainly thought so, and took her for his partner in dances as often as he could when the piper started playing. Lily was pleased, for she loved Bill and knew that he wanted to marry her.

The dancing had just begun when a beggar came to the door and asked if he might join in the fun. They called him the Gaberlunzie Man. He was a very merry fellow,

63

with a peacock's feather sticking out of his cap and a bundle over his shoulder. Willie Hume gave him a tankard of ale to drink, and soon he was dancing like a frantic daddy-long-legs; kissing the girls, teasing the old folk, and leaping high in the air shouting, "Hooch! Hooch!" He called for more and more dances till the piper was exhausted. Then the Gaberlunzie Man took the pipes and played so gaily, so rantingly, that the dancers seemed to get new feet, twirling and leaping, twisting and turning and shouting their fun and joy. When they had to stop because they were out of breath, the beggar was beside Lily, and noticed that she looked sad.

"What ails ye, lass?" he asked kindly.

"You see that very handsome lad in the blue coat? We want to marry but my father will not let us, because Bill is poor." The company was sitting down now, being too tired to do anything else. But the Gaberlunzie Man was not tired, and he sang songs and told them stories that had them all kinked with laughing.

"Isn't he great?" they said to each other.

"Never a better man did I see in all my life," said Farmer Hume. But suddenly, above the sound of laughter was heard the trampling of horse's hooves, and there strode into the barn the King's Messenger and seven knights.

"Silence!" roared the Messenger. He need not have done so, for everyone was quiet with fear. "A beggar, a Gaberlunzie Man, has this day stolen the King's silver mace. He snatched it from the bearer's hands when it was being carried in procession through the streets of Dundee, and *that*," he said pointing to the beggar, "is the man." Nobody believed such a cheery, friendly fellow could be a thief, and they all shouted, "Leave him alone. We don't believe you! We will not allow him to be taken."

"Search his bundle," ordered the Messenger. The beggar himself opened the bundle and took out — the silver mace! But he did not look the least ashamed.

"My name's Wat Wilson," he shouted. "I am the King of Beggars, why should I not have a mace?" He whirled it round his head, crying to the knights, "Come and get it!" The crowd yelled approval.

"We'll defend you," said William Hume, and told the guests to get rakes, spades, hayforks and flails. "We will save our jolly friend," he said. The guests agreed and whacked around with any tools they could find.

"He is my guest," said Willie to the Messenger, "and a better man I never saw."

"He is a thief," said the King's men, and fought as best they could, but they were beaten to the back of the barn, and the crowd was by the big door — they opened it, dashed out and locked it, with the Messenger and knights imprisoned inside.

The Gaberlunzie Man seized the pipes, and with the mace tucked under one arm and the pipes under the other, he strutted round the barn playing a gay march.

He stopped to shout through the keyhole, "You see, I have loyal people to defend me, and you are beaten, but I am a kind man, and when I see the King, I will tell him that ye did no sae badly." Then he jumped on to one of the knight's horses and galloped away.

Willie and his guests went into the farmhouse. Lily was crying, and his wife said, "Man, you're completely daft. What *have* you done? We shall be *terribly* punished. You have fought against the King's men. You surely will be hanged."

"Yet that Gaberlunzie Man was a fine fellow," he said.

The next morning there was a loud knocking at the farm door, and there was the King's Messenger (for he had broken down the barn door and escaped).

"William Hume," he announced, "you are commanded to the Royal Court by order of His Grace, James King of Scots. You may bring your daughter, for the King likes a bonny face, and your wife."

"I will go too," said Bill Kerr, with his arm round Lily. Mistress Hume was crying for she was certain her husband would be hanged.

When they arrived they were led into the Great Hall at the Palace, and there sat His Grace, James King of Scots, in his royal robes, surrounded by his knights.

"William Hume of Cairnkebbie, stand forth," roared the Messenger, and trembling Willie stood before the King.

"Of what is this man guilty?" asked the King.

"He is guilty of having fought against your Grace's knights in defence of a thief."

"Is this true, William Hume?" asked the King.

"Yes, Your Grace."

"Why did you defend such a fellow?"

"He was such a jolly man — he danced like a fly on a hot griddle, he sang, he piped, he told tales, such as —" and Willie retold one of the Gaberlunzie Man's stories so that the King and all the people in the Court were laughing. The King laughed loudest of all.

"Well, gentlemen," he said to his knights, "you bet me that I could not get my people to defend me against you. Have I won my wager?"

"Yes sire, you win," the knights said. William Hume was too frightened to listen.

"You know what the punishment is for such a crime, Willie?" said the King.

"I suppose I will lose my head," murmured Willie.

"I will now," said the King solemnly, "put on my cap to pronounce your sentence." There was silence in the Court, and Willie looked up at the King, to see, on His Grace's head, the selfsame cap as the Gaberlunzie Man had worn, with its peacock feather sticking out of it, and in his hand the silver mace!

"Was I not a jolly beggar?" said the King. "Well, Willie, I will let you go free if you agree at once to the marriage of your daughter to Bill Kerr, to whom I am giving a present of money and land for a wedding gift, and also that you will not tell people who the beggar was at your Harvest feast. Moreover, you will not need in the future to pay rent, as I give to you for your own, freely and forever, the lands and farm of Cairnkebbie."

The next feast in the barn was at the wedding of Lily and Bill Kerr, and though it was a very happy occasion, the guests were saying how much better it would have been had that joyous beggar, the Gaberlunzie Man, been with them.

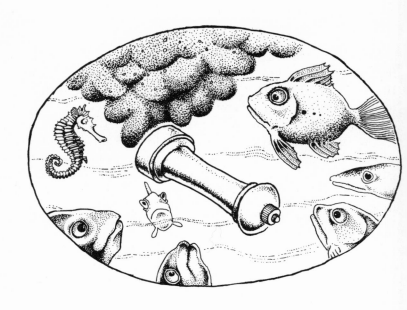

13. The Salt Sea

"Good luck to the fishing lines," said Effie, as she saw her husband putting on his oilskin coat to go fishing. Indeed, her wish came true, for Martin returned in the late summer evening with a large basket full of freshly caught herring.

"When you have packed them in salt, we shall still have not only plenty for our own needs all winter, but also lots over to sell."

Effie went to find the pack of salt. When she lifted it she was horrified, for there was only a wee bit left at the bottom of the sack.

"Martin," she called, "there's nae salt!"

"What? Nae salt? Mercy! What'll we do? All the fish will go bad, and we shall have nothing for winter meals and no money from selling the fish. Are you *sure* the sack is empty?"

"Look for yourself," she said, flinging the sack at his

feet. Martin saw that the bad news was true. "You'll need to gang to the town and get some at once," said his wife.

"It's an awful long way," grumbled Martin, but he put on his boots and started off. Before he had gone far, he met an old man whose eyes were red, whose ears were long, and whose boots were of a strange shape.

"You're looking very fashed[1]," he said to Martin.

"I've a long journey to go, to fetch salt from the town, for I have had good fishing and we have a lot to salt — but the salt sack is empty," explained Martin.

"Don't worry," said the stranger, "I'll lend you my hand mill."

"What's the use of a mill when we haven't the salt to grind?" asked Martin crossly.

"Look among those stones beside you," said the man, "and you'll find the mill." Martin did not believe him, but he turned over some of the stones and found the mill.

"Say these words after me," said the stranger, and when Martin had done so, the mill suddenly began to grind and salt poured out.

"Say what I say," said the man, and when Martin repeated the new words, the mill stopped. He was so excited he ran home with the mill under his arm.

"Why are you back so soon," demanded his wife.

"See what I've got — a mill!"

"What's the use of a mill without salt to grind, you gowk!" Then she saw that salt was pouring out of the mill like sand, and rushed to get sacks and basins and bags and boxes. As soon as they were all full, Martin remembered the words to stop the mill and it was still.

It was not long before Effie's niece came to the door to ask if her aunt could spare some salt, and got a big basin full to carry away. She told other people that there was plenty of salt for the asking at her aunt's croft, and after that people were coming continually for salt.

[1] troubled

Martin and Effie were tired of it, they had salted all the herring and were adding salt to all the food they ate, which gave Martin a terrible thirst, and that is why he went on a visit to his old friend Donald, where he could get a long drink of home-made ale. When they had drunk plenty, Donald asked for the loan of the mill, 'just for a day or two,' and Martin was glad to be rid of it. Donald thought he would sell salt to the other fishermen, who would put it with the fish into barrels to keep it fresh to eat in winter. In this way, Donald expected to make quite a lot of money. He was so excited, that having learnt the words to start the mill, he forgot to ask for the ones that would stop it.

Martin went home, and Donald was left with the mill grinding away. He fetched bags and sacks and boxes, and when they were full, the mill kept on grinding and the salt fell on to the floor, and still more came and more came; it was feet deep on the floor, it put out the fire, it rose as high as the windowsill, and Donald was saying every word he could think of to try and stop it, but nothing was any use and he could only shout, "Stop it! Stop it!" which made no difference, the mill still kept pouring out salt.

The door was nearly blocked when the Captain of the fishing fleet called to see if he could get some salt. Donald offered him sacks full, but the Captain did not want to carry such a burden and he asked for the loan of the mill. He did not ask how to stop it, for he did not want it to stop, he would fill his ship and sell the salt abroad. So he staggered away with the mill under his arm and the salt streeling on the path as he went.

He filled the hold of his ship, but soon the deck and even the cabins were full of salt. The crew became afraid the ship would sink.

"Throw that thing away!" they shouted.

"You shall share the money we will make selling the

salt abroad," offered the Captain. But the ship was getting low in the water with the weight of the salt.

"We're sinking! The ship is sinking!" shouted the crew, and they took no notice of the Captain, but flung the mill overboard, where it sank to the bottom of the sea, and there it kept on grinding and grinding, and is still grinding, which is why the sea is salt.

14. Whuppity Stoorie

"Why do you keep going out to look at the pig?" Jamie asked his mother.

"Well lad," she replied, "I am expecting the pig to have piglets, and indeed that is good because we can sell the wee pigs and so have money to pay the rent for this cottage."

"What if the pig doesn't give us any baby pigs?"

"Oh Jamie, she *must*, or we could not pay the rent and would have nowhere to live or sleep."

Now Jamie was worried too. Their cottage was in a lonely place surrounded by woods, and as he cuddled down in bed that night he wondered what it would be like to have nowhere to sleep, except among all those dark trees in the wood. Certainly, bright moonlight was shining through the small window of his room, but if they were in the wood, moonlight would bring all sorts of animals out hunting, badgers and foxes, and just then an owl

72

hooted and Jamie hid his head under the blankets. He heard his mother go out again to the pig-sty.

She was remembering that the man who owned the cottage had told her, "Mrs. MacKay, you must pay the rent before the end of the month." It was nearly the end of the month now, and she had no money. She lit the lantern and went out to look at the pig. "It will be all right," she thought. "There will be at least five or six wee piglets and I will be able to pay the rent. Jamie and I are very happy in this little house. The pig will be all right."

But the pig was *not* all right. It lay on its side peching[1] and moaning and frothing at the mouth.

"God help us, it's dying!" said Mrs. MacKay. "What will I do? No piglets, no rent, no rent, no house!" and she flung her apron over her head while she cried.

Just then, she heard a voice nearby, saying "What's wrong?" Who could it be, so near, so late? She dropped her apron and was amazed to see a nicely dressed old lady beside her.

"It's the pig," she said to the lady, "it's dying and that means no piglets, no piglets means no rent, no rent means no house. Oh! I'd give *anything* to see the pig right again!"

"Indeed! Would you give *anything*? If you keep that promise, I'll make the pig well again, and it will have piglets and you will be able to pay the rent, and keep your house."

"Oh please, please, I'll give you *anything*." The old lady leaned over the wall of the pigsty and touched the pig. It grunted, flicked its ears and stood up.

"You go to bed," said the old lady to Mrs. MacKay, "the piglets will be here in the morning." Mrs. MacKay went back into the cottage. She looked at Jamie, asleep and dreaming happily, and then went to bed herself. When she wakened in the morning she went straight to the pig-sty, and there was the pig with ten lovely piglets.

[1] panting

"Come and look," she shouted to Jamie, but she did not say anything about the old lady. Indeed she began to wonder if it had only been a dream.

"Now we won't need to sleep in the wood," said Jamie. Mrs. MacKay took the piglets to market, got a good price and paid the rent. She bought food and a book for Jamie; she was teaching him to read, for she wanted him to grow up a very clever man. Next day she was busy baking and Jamie was reading his book, when there was a knock on the door and there stood the old lady.

"You made a promise," she said. "You said you would give *anything* if I made the pig well. You've got your piglets and you've paid the rent. Now I claim what I want."

"Indeed yes, I am grateful," said Mrs. MacKay. "What would you like? I can give you a lovely pair of blankets."

"I don't want blankets," said the old woman crossly.

"I can give you a very good lamp."

"I don't want a lamp."

"I can give you a beautiful brooch. It belonged to my grandmother and has a lovely pebble —"

"I don't want a brooch."

"Well, what *do* you want?"

"I want the bairn, Jamie."

"Oh no no no! You can't have Jamie!" cried Mrs. MacKay, clutching her son in her arms.

"I shall come for him tomorrow," said the old woman, and disappeared. Both Jamie and his mother were too frightened to sleep that night.

"Don't let her take me!" Jamie cried.

"No no, little son. I will think of something else to give her." But his mother knew that she really did not possess anything else of great value to offer, and sure enough next morning there was the old woman at the door. Mrs. Mackay held Jamie tight.

"I'll take the laddie now," said the old lady with a nasty grin.

"No, you can't have my son," cried Mrs. MacKay. "I'll do *anything* for you instead. What can I do for you?"

"Well, I'll give you once chance," said the old lady. "If by this time tomorrow you can tell me what is my name, I won't take the boy." She gave a cruel laugh and was gone.

Her name? Her name? What could it be? She looked wealthy. Could it be Elspeth? Euphemia? Anne? It could be Betty, Janet or Kate. It could be — oh, what could it be! Mrs. MacKay could not cook nor sew nor wash nor bake. She could only keep repeating names.

Supposing she could not guess the right name? It might be something magical that she had never heard of, and then Jamie, her darling little son, would be taken away from her for ever. She went to take another look at him fast asleep in his cot. She could not sleep herself, she could not even go to bed, so she went for a stroll in the wood. It was very quiet, and she sat down to rest on a slab of stone. Could the name be Tabitha? Could it be Mildred? Then she thought she heard the sound of a spinning wheel. How could it be a spinning wheel in the wood? It seemed to come from under the stone on which she sat. She looked down and saw a small hole. She peeped through it and saw the same old lady busy spinning and singing, and this is what she sang:

> "Little kens the goodwife at hame
> That Whuppity Stoorie is my name."

Mrs. MacKay could have shouted for joy, but she kept quiet and crept away home, whispering to herself, "Whuppity Stoorie, Whuppity Stoorie," over and over again in case she should forget it.

Next morning the old lady came to the cottage. Jamie was playing on the doorstep.

"You're coming with me. Ha! Ha!" the old lady said.

"No, no," cried Jamie hiding behind his mother's skirt.

75

"Yes, you are coming with me because your mother does not know my name."

Of course Mrs. MacKay had not forgotten the name she had heard, but she thought she would tease the old wretch.

"It's Nellie," she said.

"No, it's not."

"It's Janet."

"No, it's not."

"It's Kate."

"No, it's not," said the old lady, making a grab at Jamie.

"It's Whuppity Stoorie," shouted Mrs. MacKay. The old dame let go of Jamie and went red in the face with anger.

"Who told you?" she said, stamping her foot.

"You told me yourself," laughed Mrs. MacKay, and as she lifted Jamie up in her arms the old lady disappeared.

"What a funny name," said Jamie. And it was, wasn't it?

15. Mac a Rusgaich

There was a farmer standing at the market looking for a man to work for him. He was little and mean in his mind and was seeking for one who would be foolish enough not to ask for big wages. He saw a lad standing with a straw in his mouth, which meant that he was not yet engaged by a master.

"I am needing a man," said the farmer. "Will you work for me?"

"If you are a good master, I will work for you. But what will you want me to do?"

"You will have the peats to foot, and you will have to herd the mountain moor, and hold the plough."

"I will do all that."

"The bargain is that you must do exactly as I say."

"I will, but you must not ask me to do more than I am able, or I must get double wages from you."

"Very good, I agree to that. What is your name?"

"Mac a Rusgaich."

So Mac a Rusgaich went to his new home and he did not think much of his room, for it was so small that when he put his trousers on, his feet were out of the window. As for his bed, there was less straw to it than the cattle had to lie on in the byre.

The first morning he rose and asked what was to be his task, and was told to go and foot the peats.

"Well," he said to the farmer's wife, "I must have my breakfast first."

She gave him his breakfast, but his porridge bowl was as small as a cat's saucer, and the milk had no cream on it at all.

"You had best give me my dinner now as well," said Mac a Rusgaich, "then I need not waste my time coming home for it from the peat bog in the middle of the day."

The farmer's wife was not pleased, but she was in a hurry to see the heels of him, so she gave him his dinner. What was there to it but a tiny piece of meat holding on to a large bone, and one potato, and it left Mac a Rusgaich still hungry.

"If you will be giving me my supper now, I will not need to be bothering you any more to-day for food," he said.

Hoping to be rid of him at last, she threw his supper at him, and what was it but a bowl of soup no bigger than a baby's mouth. But Mac a Rusgaich was satisfied that with breakfast, dinner and supper all together he had had one good meal from his mean master.

"Tell me," he asked when he had finished, "what do your servants do when they have finished their supper?"

"What should they do but go to bed?" she replied with anger running to her head. But if the small anger was on her then, it was the big anger when she saw Mac a Rusgaich go to his bed and lie down. She fetched her husband.

78

When the farmer came and saw the lad in bed he roared, "What are you doing there? Have I not told you to go out and foot the peats?"

"Tomorrow maybe I will go," said Mac a Rusgaich, "but I cannot go now for I have had my breakfast, my dinner and my supper, and your wife says that your servants go to bed when they have had their supper." And he lay in bed that day.

The next morning the master shouted at him, "Away with you to the plough as I told you, fool!" And Mac a Rusgaich rose and went to the plough.

After a while the farmer went round to the field to see how the new lad was getting on with the ploughing, and there was the field without one single ribbon of brown on its green dress, and the man standing at the plough and no horses to pull it!

"What are you doing, you fool, standing there holding the handles of the plough and no horses in it? Will that plough the field?"

"You did not say I would be asked to plough, but only that I must 'hold the plough', and I am holding it."

The master was black angry, but what could he say except, "It is true that I said those words." He thought that perhaps the lad would be better at working on the hill.

"Will you go up the hill to herd as we agreed?"

"Yes, I will go as we agreed."

"There should be fourteen stirks and five heifers up there."

Most of the day was behind the hill before Mac a Rusgaich returned.

"Were the cattle all there?" asked the farmer.

"I don't know."

"Indeed you were not there when good sense was given out, but you are in the wrong this time, for you did agree to herd the mountain moor."

"I did, and I have herded it. I made sure that the

mountain moor was there and that it would stay there. That is herding it."

There was red anger on the master, but what could he say, except, "Well, it is true I said those words."

At last he went to look for the beasts himself. It was many steps this way and that way with the master and his dog looking for the cattle, and back home he came to say that three of the cattle were missing.

"Get away with you and look for them," he shouted at Mac a Rusgaich.

"Where will I look for them?"

"Oh! Go and look for them where you think they might be, and then where you think they might not be. I've looked in every hole that *I* can think of."

Being very weary he went into the house and sat down to refreshment with his wife. Soon there was a noise upon the roof, and soon thatch began to fly past the window, and soon dirt poured on the floor from above, and soon the face of Mac a Rusgaich was showing through a hole in the roof.

"He is pulling the thatch off the roof! Stop it, you fool, stop it! What do you think you are doing?"

"Well, master, I looked for the cattle where I thought they might be, and now I am looking for them where I thought they might not be."

The master was as full of white anger as a bed of nettles, but he was determined that he would get some work from this fool of a man. But what could he say except, "Well, it is true I said those words."

He thought he would tell Mac a Rusgaich to do something that had not been mentioned before and then he could not make a mistake.

"Go and clean and wash the horses, and the stable, inside and out." Mac a Rusgaich was a very long time, and the farmer was expecting well groomed horses and a very clean stable, inside and out.

MAC A RUSGAICH

In came Mac a Rusgaich, saying, "I have finished."

"Good then. That is one thing you have done rightly, and now away and put the horses into the plough." The lad was soon back this time.

"Have you put the horses into the plough?"

"The horses won't listen to me. They won't get up."

"Won't they? I'll soon get them up." But he could not get them up, for Mac a Rusgaich had killed them.

"I did exactly as you told me," he said. "You told me to clean and wash the horses and the stable inside and out. How could I wash the horses inside without killing them?"

"You fool, you fool!" The master was mad with rage, but what could he say, but, "It is true that I said those words, but get you away from here, and you shall not have any wages."

"Indeed but you must give me double wages for you have asked me to do more than I was able, and that was, to do much work without good food in me."

But the master would not give him any wages and raised his stick to beat Mac a Rusgaich. So the lad went to the chief of his clan and told his tale, and the chief went to the farmer and made him give double wages. Thus the farmer had more to pay than if the small meanness had not been in him, and he offered to the next man that came to work for him a good wage and plenty of food.

16. The Magic Milking Stool

Mairi was beautiful. She really was, and she knew it. She was often looking in the mirror to make sure that her lovely curls were in place, and putting her head on one side to look coy. She knew that the boys all thought her beautiful. Perhaps it is not surprising that she became really conceited, and thought she should not be sweeping the floor or washing dishes or herding the cattle on the hill. "Stupid beasts," she said, and would give them a whack with a stick. The cattle did not understand what it was all about and just went their own quiet way, and that annoyed Mairi still more.

One day, bringing the cows back to the byre to milk them, she was especially grumpy, for it was hot and she was tired.

"I should be in a grand house with servants to work for me," she said, "and I should have necklaces to show off

82

ny nice neck, and bracelets to show off my hands," and
he whacked the biggest cow hard. "Get on," she said.
"Why should I bother milking you?" Then she heard
someone call "Mairi!" and saw an old woman walking
behind her.

"Wait a minute, Mairi. I have something for you," she
said. Mairi hoped it would be a pretty piece of lace or a bit
of bright ribbon, but what the woman held out was a wee
milking stool. Mairi pouted.

"Couldn't you do the milking for me?" she asked hopefully.

"We'll see about that," said the woman with a smile.
They went into the byre and when she had tied the cows
up, Mairi sat on the wee stool and started to milk, but to
her surprise she did not need to use her hands, for the milk
just came pouring into the milk pail and it was full in a
minute! She went to the next cow, and the same thing
happened, and to the next, and each time she did not need
to do anything, the milk just poured into the buckets.

"How is this happening?" she asked the old woman.

"It's a magic milking stool, my dear."

"Can I have it for always?" Mairi asked hopefully.

"Only if you will make a promise to me, and keep it."

"Goodness yes, I'll promise almost anything," said Mairi,
thinking that with the milking so quickly done, she would
be able to go to the village and be complimented by her
admirers. "What is it you want?"

"You must promise," said the old lady, "not to hit the
cattle any more, you are very rough and unkind to them.
It doesn't matter what you say to them, but you must not
hit them. If you hurt them, the little stool will know what
to do, and you will be sorry."

"Oh that's easy," said Mairi, and for the next few days,
whenever she used the stool it did the milking for her, and
she could spend the evenings putting on her best shoes and
dresses and going around to be looked at, especially by

Iain and Alasdair, the shepherd's sons. But she still though
she should not do housework or peel the potatoes.

Then one day the cows had fed well on the hill and wer
in no hurry; they stopped on the way to the byre to snatc
at specially green tufts of grass, and walked slowly, mooin
sometimes and looking about.

"Get on you stupid things," cried Mairi, and picking u
a piece of wood, she hit them hard — really hard, so tha
they ran the last few yards. Mairi took the little milkin
stool into the byre and sat on it to watch the milk flov
into the pail, but no sooner was she seated, than the stoc
began to dance up and down, and she found that she coul
not stand up. She was stuck to it! This was dreadful. Bum
bump bump she went, up and down, while the stoc
joggled her out of the byre door, and jog jog bump bum
right into the village, where it danced round the cottage
and everyone came out to see and to laugh. Mairi's shoe
fell off, her hair was all loose and tangled, her face was red
and bump bump went the stool out of the village into th
country where brambles scratched her face and bracke
scarred her legs, then it jogged away right up to the moo
where it tossed her into the heather and disappeared.

Barefoot and bleeding and crying, she ran home, bu
stopped on the way at the pool in the burn to wash he
face and arms in the cool water. When she saw her face a
scratched and dirty reflected in the pool and her hair ful
of twigs, she could not help laughing, and when she go
home and looked more closely in the mirror, she laughe
still more. When she went again into the village, Iain an
Alasdair the shepherd's sons could not stop looking at he

"How much prettier she is now," said Iain, "she i
lovely when she laughs instead of frowning and pouting."

"Right enough," said Alasdair, "and she is singing al
day too. I'm going to marry her."

"Oh no you're not, for I intend to marry her." Indee
plenty of men now wanted to marry Mairi the merry gir
and she could choose whichever one she wanted.

17. The Sisters

ere were two sisters, Cathie and Anne, and they were so
nd of each other that they always went about hand in
nd; they told each other their secrets and shared any-
ing they had. But there was one thing that they did *not*
together. Cathie got up every morning to go into their
rden to wash her face in the morning dew, which made
r very, very beautiful. Anne was a sleepy-head, and
ough she was proud to have such a beautiful sister, she
d not mind how she looked herself. Her mother used to
se Cathie.

"If you get up too early," she would say, "the Wizard
ll take you." But Cathie only laughed, and was always
at sunrise and washing her face in the morning dew.
en Cathie would come back to bed with cold feet,
ne would complain, "Keep your cold feet away from
."

But one morning Cathie did not come back. Anne g[e]
up for breakfast.

"Where's Cathie?" said her mother.

"She's not back from the garden yet," said Anne. "I
go and fetch her." But Anne could not find her sister.
was a big garden, and she looked through all the flowe[r]
beds and among the vegetables and the gooseberries an[d]
the blackcurrant bushes, but Cathie was not there. Present[ly]
her mother, and then her father came to hunt for her, b[ut]
Cathie was not there.

"She must have gone out to the moor," her father sai[d]
and away he went to look for her.

"I am afraid some magic has happened to her," said th[e]
mother when her husband came back.

"She is not on the moor," he said.

"I shall go and look for her," said Anne, "no matt[er]
how far away she has gone, I shall find her."

"No, no," said her mother. "If you go something will ha[p]
pen to you too." But Anne was so worried that she could n[ot]
sleep, she could not eat, and grew so thin and ill that at la[st]
her mother said, "I suppose you must go, but I will give y[ou]
some things to bring you luck on the journey. She made up [a]
bundle of food and also gave Anne a gold coin, a gold need[le]
a packet of pins, a silver thimble and a small sharp knife.

Anne set off, going over the hills round about whe[re]
they lived, asking everyone if they had seen Cathie. S[he]
went miles and miles away from home.

"Have you seen a lovely girl with red hair and brow[n]
eyes?" she would ask. But nobody had seen her sister. [So]
Anne walked away up into the Highlands. She was a b[it]
afraid of the high mountains, but she would not give [up]
looking for her sister. "I *must* find her," she kept sayi[ng]
to herself.

One day she met a wandering singer. He seemed [to]
have lost something, for he was searching all around [on]
the ground.

"Have you seen a very beautiful girl with red hair and brown eyes?" she asked, not feeling very hopeful.

"I believe I have," he said surprisingly, "but she was taken away by the Wizard who has locked her up in his castle. I'm afraid you will never see her again."

"Oh, but I'll go and see the Wizard," said Anne.

"Then you'll get locked up too," said the singer.

"Well, I'm going to try anyway," said Anne. "How do I find the Wizard?"

"You see that hill? It's called Mischanter Hill, and the Wizard's castle is at the top of it."

"It looks very steep," said Anne, but the singer made no reply, he was still busy searching the ground for something.

"What have you lost?" Anne asked.

"I've lost a penny, the only thing I earned today."

"Oh dear, that doesn't seem much. Take this coin that my mother gave me," and she handed him the gold coin.

"Goodness!" exclaimed the singer, "I wouldn't earn as much as that in a year! May I give you in return a piece of advice? Remember, when you are in the castle, that *things are not as they seem.*"

"What do you mean?" asked Anne, but the stranger was already running away.

Anne climbed on up the hill, when she saw an old man sitting by the path. He had a whistle in his hand, and kept shaking it.

"Can't you play on your whistle?" asked Anne, for she felt a tune would cheer her.

"Something has got stuck in it," said the man sadly.

"See if this is any help," said Anne, holding out the gold needle that her mother had given her. The man pushed the needle into the whistle, and then put it to his lips and blew.

"That's fine," he said smiling. "That's cleared it." He played a cheery tune. "Where are you going?"

"I'm going to the castle at the top of the hill to try to find my sister."

"It's a bad Wizard lives there," he warned her. "Will you remember to *take three?*"

"Take three," repeated Anne. "Whatever does that mean?" But the old man was already on his way down the hill, playing a merry tune. She had climbed quite a long way up the hill when she met a beggar woman. She must be very poor, Anne thought, for her clothes were so worn and torn that she had tried to hold them together with thorns.

"What a pity I gave away the gold needle," Anne thought, "but the needle would have been no use without thread. Anyway, I have the pins."

"Stand still," she said to the woman, "I will pin some of these rents with pins my mother gave me." The beggar woman was very pleased.

"Where are you going, lassie?" she asked.

"I am going to the Wizard's castle to try and find my sister."

"Oh dear! I wouldn't do that, he'll eat you."

"I must find my sister," said Anne.

"Well, my dear, remember to *try silver*," said the beggar woman.

"Try silver," repeated Anne. "I wonder what that means." She went climbing on up the mountain.

At last she was facing the great black castle. It looked so dreadful she would have liked to turn back; it had no windows, only a huge wooden door. But she thought of her poor sister shut up there with the wicked Wizard and banged on the door. It was immediately flung open, and she stepped inside and faced the Wizard. What a horrible face he had! Great big teeth and eyes that glared like lamps.

"Ho! Ho!" he roared, "so you've come to find your sister?"

"Yes — yes," stammered Anne, trembling.

"Wait here," said the Wizard, and left her in the big hall. There was no sound, and then she smelt burning. She heard the crackle of flames, and the place filled with smoke that made her cough and her eyes burn. Then suddenly, all round her was a ring of flame. She saw a door, but she could not get to it through the flames; then she remembered the singer's words, *things are not as they seem*.

"Maybe the fire is not what it seems," thought Anne, and bravely stepped forward. The flames did not burn her, and she dashed through the door on to a passage. She heard the Wizard laugh. There were doors all along the side of the passage, and they were numbered. Anne passed the first, she passed the second, for she did not know what might be behind them, and then she remembered the whistler's advice, *take three*, and wondering what she would see, she opened the third door.

She saw a great hall filled with statues on pedestals, and every statue was exactly like Cathie. Could one possibly be the real Cathie? Anne wondered what she should do. Each person she had met had given her good advice. What was it the beggar woman had said? Oh yes, she had said *try silver*, and Anne remembered the silver thimble her mother had given her. She took it from her pocket. Thimbles are for fingers, so she put it on a finger of the nearest statue. Nothing happened, except that the thimble went black. She tried it on the next statue and nothing happened, except that the thimble went black again.

"Oh dear! They must *all* be statues!" she moaned. "Cathie, which one is *you*?" But the statues were all still and silent. "I will try *once* more," said Anne, and placed the silver thimble on the third statue. It did not turn black, and the hand moved. Anne looked anxiously up at the face, which smiled, the cheeks turned rosy, the hair on the head went soft and silky, and Cathie stepped down from the pedestal and stood beside her sister. They were too

89

frightened to move in case the Wizard should appear, and spoke in whispers. But the Wizard did not seem to be near, for he had not expected Anne to have changed Cathie from the statue.

"Come!" whispered Anne, and the sisters escaped out of the big castle door and ran as fast as they could down the mountain path. But the Wizard heard them, and was soon striding after them; they could feel his evil-smelling hot breath, and soon his terrible face was glaring at them in anger, and his hands with their huge claws were almost on their backs.

"Run, run, Cathie!" shouted Anne.

"Can't," puffed Cathie, and indeed, neither could Anne. It seemed as if the Wizard would just pick them up and eat them, but as his face came close to Anne's, she took the little sharp knife from her pocket and drove it into the hideous mouth. There was a flash like blue lightning, a roar and a scream, and the whole castle came tumbling down. The great stones rolled past them, covering them with dust, but at first they were too frightened to look. Suddenly there was silence and everything was still, and when they opened their eyes, there was nothing to be seen on the top of the hill — no wizard, no castle — but they could hear the singer and the whistler making happy music.

Soon they were home, being hugged and kissed by their parents, and Anne telling all that had happened.

"What a brave girl you were," said Cathie. "The Wizard took me when I was washing my face in the morning dew." And never again did Cathie do that, but washed her face as you and I do, with soap and water.

18. Diarmaid

There were three great warriors, Fionn, Ossian and Diarmaid, and they were camping on the side of a mountain. The weather was bad, with wind and snow, when a woman called at the closed tent of Fionn, and asked that she might have shelter.

"Come in," said Fionn, but when he saw her he was surprised and angry. "You are horribly ugly," he said, "your uncombed hair is down to your knees, your lips are wrinkled and your eyes screwed. Get away." The woman looked at him angrily, but she went, and she stood outside the tent of Ossian.

"The night is wild," she called, "let me in for shelter."

"Come in," said Ossian, and then he turned and looked at her. "Did I ever see an uglier woman?" he exclaimed. "Your untidy hair is to your knees, your face is wrinkled, your hands like claws, how dare you disturb me? Go away,

91

old hag!" The woman looked hard at him, but she went, and she stood outside the tent of Diarmaid.

"It is a terrible night," she called. "Let me in."

"Indeed it is a wild night," said Diarmaid, "come in." The woman stood before him. "Indeed you are not comely, but you are cold, poor thing. Come under the blanket," he said, and the woman came and lay beside him. He was not asleep, and she looked at him, seeing that he was the handsomest of all the warriors of Scotland. She bent her head towards him.

"Kiss me, Diarmaid," she said. Now Diarmaid did not want to kiss that ugly old mouth, but he felt sorry for a woman so old and lonely and he kissed her. As he raised his face, he saw that she had turned into the most beautiful woman; her long hair was golden, her skin smooth as ripe fruit, her eyes like stars and her arms and limbs plump and lovely.

In the morning, they stepped out of the tent together to take breakfast with the other two.

"Diarmaid!" said Fionn. "Where did you get so lovely a wife?"

"I am looking at the most beautiful woman in the world!" said Ossian. "Where did she come from?"

"You refused me shelter last night when I looked old," said the lady. Fionn and Ossian were mad with themselves that they had turned her away.

That night, she said to Diarmaid, "If you had a lovely castle, where would you like it to be built?"

"Right on the top of this very hill," said Diarmaid.

When he wakened in the morning, he looked out of the tent to see what the weather would be like for hunting, and there he saw a magnificent castle on the top of the hill.

"It is yours," said his wife, "let us go and live in it."

Diarmaid could hardly believe all the lovely things they found in the castle. Gold tables covered with the most luscious food and drink; beautiful curtains and soft beds with sheets of silk and, what Diarmaid liked most of all, a greyhound that had three puppies. But after a while he became restless.

"You are missing your companions, Fionn and Ossian," said his wife.

"I am missing hunting with them," he admitted.

"Then go you to the hunt with them," she said. And he gathered his hunting gear and was going out of the gates of the castle, when the greyhound came forward and licked his hand.

"Look after the hound and her three pups," he called to his wife. "Don't let any ill befall them."

"I will do that," she said. "But, Diarmaid, I want you to promise that whatever happens, you will never remind me what I looked like when you first saw me."

"I will never do that, beloved wife," he promised, and went off to join his companions. They were away a long time, hunting deer and duck and camping out, but at last Diarmaid longed for his beautiful wife and made up his mind to leave his companions and return to the castle.

But one day, not long after he had gone, a stranger came to the castle gate, where Diarmaid's wife was playing with the greyhound and the three pups.

"Will you come in and have some refreshment?" she invited the guest.

"I am not hungry nor thirsty," he said, "but I would so very much like to have one of those pups." As there were three, the wife thought one could be spared, so she gave one to the visitor, and he went away.

A few days later another visitor came to the castle, and again she offered the best refreshment, but all the visitor wanted was one of the greyhound's pups. "There will still be one left," she thought, and gave him the second pup.

Two days before Diarmaid would be returning, a third visitor came to the castle, and he too wanted a pup.

"I cannot let you have it," said Diarmaid's wife. "It is

the only one left, and my husband would be angry if I gave it to you." But he was a nice young man, and he pleaded so hard with her, that at last she agreed and he took the pup.

Diarmaid came home, and the first thing he saw as he approached the castle was the greyhound, alone and looking very sad.

"Where are the pups?" he demanded, and his wife told him she had given the three pups to the three visitors.

Diarmaid was very angry. He was so angry that he said, "You have forgotten what an ugly old hag you were when I took you in that night on the mountain!"

"Diarmaid," she said, looking at him sadly, "you promised you would never remind me of that!"

"I beg your pardon," he said.

That night, he was stroking the head of the greyhound. "She misses her pups," he said, "you should not have taken them from her."

"You are making too much fuss about those pups," said his wife.

"I told you when I went away to take care of them," he retorted angrily, "you should do as I say, you have forgotten the night I gave you shelter when you were an ugly, nasty old woman."

"Diarmaid," she reminded him, "you promised you would never remind me of that, and you have done so twice."

"I beg your pardon," he said, "I forgot."

Next day they were going for a walk in the forest, the greyhound with them.

"If the three pups had been here," said Diarmaid, "they would have been learning to hunt."

"Can't you forget those silly pups?" she said.

"No, I can't, because you promised to look after them while I was away. You would have been more careful if you had remembered what you looked like when I gave you shelter that night of the storm —" and before he could

94

finish the sentence, the castle had disappeared, his wife was gone and the greyhound lay dead at his feet. He was sorry indeed that he had forgotten his promise, and had three times reminded his lovely wife of how she had looked when he took her in. He set out to find her.

"No person, and no peril shall prevent me from finding my beloved," he said. He went to look for her among the islands, and searching on one of them he saw a lass cutting rushes.

"For what use are you cutting those rushes?" he asked.

"They are for my mistress, the Princess, she needs them to lie on, for she has been ill for many a day."

"Take me to her," demanded Diarmaid.

"How can I do that? The King would kill me if he found out, besides, there are sentries."

"Bundle me in among the rushes," suggested Diarmaid, "and carry me on your back."

"What, a great lump like you? You are far too heavy," she laughed. But Diarmaid could persuade almost anybody to do what he wanted, and soon he was hidden inside the bundle, and being carried on the girl's back.

"You have plenty this time!" remarked a sentry.

"You are a strong lass, I believe you could carry half the rocks on the mountainside," laughed another. So Diarmaid was safely carried into the castle, and right into the Princess's room. It was such a happy surprise that she felt better at once, but not yet *quite* well, she told him. Diarmaid was always kind to ladies, so he asked, "What else do you need?"

"I need the gold cup that belongs to the King of the Plains," she said.

"And where am I to look for that?" he asked.

"The little brown man will tell you."

"And where do I find the little brown man?"

"I don't know. Go and look for him," she said crossly. So Diarmaid went to look for the little brown man, and was surprised to meet him at the castle gate.

"Where do I find the King of the Plains?" he asked.

"I will take you," said the little brown man, who looked as if he were dressed in bracken.

It was a long journey, a day and a night, and a night and a day, and on and on. Diarmaid was tired, and wished he had not offered to help the rather disagreeable Princess.

When they got to the castle of the King of the Plains, Diarmaid stood on a rock and shouted, "I have come for the golden cup."

"Have you then?" roared the King. "Then you must battle for it." So a warrior came out from the castle and did battle with Diarmaid, who enjoyed a struggle. The clash of their swords frightened every animal of hill or stream for miles around, and the little brown man was glad when it was over, and the warrior lying dead at Diarmaid's feet.

"Give me the cup," Diarmaid shouted, and the little brown man went into the castle and came out bearing the gold cup that was almost bigger than himself. Together they journeyed from sun-up to sun-down many, many times, back to the Princess. She was very pleased with the cup.

"Now you can marry me," she said, "and have half my father's kingdom."

"There is no need," said Diarmaid, "I seek my own wife."

"You will find her at home," said the little brown man quietly.

So Diarmaid returned to the mountain, and there was the castle as before, with his wife waiting at the gate.

"Have you forgiven me?" he asked. "It was unkind and rude of me to remind you of that night, and I shall never do so again."

"That is all right, Diarmaid, my dear husband," she said, and the little brown man laughed as he saw them kiss.

19. The Bracelet

Dolina lived with her uncle, who was a weaver. A mean man, he was, always grumbling that she did not spin fast enough to keep him at work at the loom, and he expected her to clean the house, cook the meals and take care of their sixteen sheep, which gave the wool for weaving. When the cloth was woven, Dolina took it to market to sell.

"Get a high price for it," he would say, "and bring me all the money, don't go buying trash for yourself." When Dolina got a good price for the cloth, she found it very difficult not to buy something for herself with some of the money, perhaps a summer dress, for hers were made up from odd bits of tweed discarded from the loom, and she longed for a pair of shoes, for she was barefoot.

One day at the market, a man was selling jewellery, and amongst it was a beautiful gold bracelet. Seeing Dolina looking at it with such interest, he told her, "That is no ordinary bracelet, dear, it comes from far Cathay and has magic powers." Dolina turned away and tried not to think of the bracelet, though there was plenty of money from the cloth in the leather bag under her arm.

The jeweller left his stall, and with the bracelet in his hand, came to speak to her.

"The bracelet has powers," he reminded her, "and I will give it to you for very little money, because I feel tnat you are going to need it." Dolina opened her money bag, paid the jeweller and slipped the bracelet on to her arm. She pushed it far up and pulled down her sleeve. For whatever happened, her uncle must not see it.

When she got home she gave him the rest of the money.

"This is less than usual," he grumbled.

"Prices were not so good today," she said.

"You had best go and see that the sheep are all right," said her uncle. So Dolina went out and stood on a small hill from which she could see their sixteen sheep. One, two, three, four, five, six, seven, eight, nine, ten, eleven, twelve, thirteen, fourteen. Where were the other two? She counted again, but only fourteen were to be seen. She searched all round about, but could not find the missing ones. So she went back to the house. Her uncle was busy at the loom.

"You've been a long time. What were you doing?" he asked crossly.

"Two sheep are missing. I was looking for them."

"Sheep missing! You young fool! How do you think I can weave without wool? Where will I get wool except from the sheep?" Dolina tried to get on with the housework. She needed to refill the water bucket from the well. As she bent down to pick up the pail, her bracelet slipped down to her wrist.

"What's that?" shouted her uncle. "What are you doing with jewellery? Where did you get it? You have been spending my money on your vanity and telling me lies!"

His face was scarlet with fury. "And you lose the sheep too, you good-for-nothing idiot! Get my dinner at once, and then out you go, and don't come back till you've found the sheep, or I'll whip the skin off you." He slapped her face and, snatching the bracelet from her arm, put it in his pocket.

She cooked his dinner and washed up the dishes, and her uncle sat by the fire and dozed off to sleep. This was Dolina's chance to get back the bracelet. She knelt at his side, terrified in case he should waken, then slowly and carefully drew the precious bracelet from his pocket and slipped it high up on her arm.

When he wakened, he went again to work at the loom.

"Go and look for those sheep," he said again, "and if you come back without having found them, I'll give you such a beating as you will remember for the rest of your life." Dolina was frightened at his angry face and left the house at once to look for the lost sheep.

She walked all over the hills, into the hidden corries and beside the streams. She counted the sheep that were there over and over again, but there were only fourteen. She looked at the house, but she dared not go back, even though it was getting near sunset. She wondered if the sheep could have gone into the wood, and took the little path that led to it. She had not gone far when she heard the sound of an axe, and came across a handsome young man chopping wood.

"Hello," he said. "Where have you come from? You look sad." Dolina told him of the lost sheep. "When I have finished this work I will come and help you to find them," he said. When he was ready, he took her hand and they set off to find the sheep.

"They might be in the cave by the shore," he suggested. So they went to the cave but found no sheep. It was getting dark.

"You had better go home," he advised her.

"No, no, I daren't. He'll half kill me."

"Well, I will stay with you," he said, and Dolina was very grateful for she was afraid. As they sat side by side in the cave, he noticed something written on the wall. They had to wait till daylight to make out what it said. Then they read, "AT THE SPINNING ROCK YOU WILL FIND IT. GO ALONE."

"That must mean where we will find the sheep. Some one must have stolen them and taken them to this Spinning Rock," said Kenneth (for that was his name).

"But if they were stolen, the thief would not say where they were," said Dolina, "and it says 'find *it*' not 'find *them*'."

"But I think you should go. I would come with you, but it says 'go alone' and it surely can't be far away."

"I shall be all right, for I have a lucky bracelet," said Dolina, and showed him the bangle.

"I must go back to my work," said Kenneth, and kissed her.

Dolina started to look for the Spinning Rock. She found a path leading from the cave, but when she came to a parting of the way, she did not know which road to go. She bent down to see if there was any sign, such as a footprint, and as she did so, the bracelet fell from her arm and ran in front of her like a little golden wheel. Away to the right she followed it, on and on till they came to a big river; its water was black and so rough that white waves were lashing about, and the roar of the rushing water was terrible.

"What can I do now?" thought Dolina, and then she saw a fragile-looking narrow wooden bridge. She was just putting her foot on it to cross, when she noticed that the bracelet was lying still. She stopped, but her foot was already caught on the wood, and with a splash she was in the torrent, being smashed this way and that, her mouth full of water, her heavy tweed dress pulling her under. She

as certain she was going to drown. How she wished
Kenneth had been with her, and that she had watched the
bracelet more carefully. As she was swept along, she
caught sight of its glistening gold on the side of the bank,
and struggled towards it. It was hanging from the low
branch of a tree over the water. With a great effort, she
reached up for the branch, and just managing to catch it,
pulled herself up on the bank. She was cold and trembling,
but the little golden wheel ran and bounced in front of
her, so that she had to run to keep up.

It came to rest outside a small shed. Dolina went in, and
there was a white pony. She got on its back, and it moved
out of the shed, towards the river, the gold bracelet
hanging from its mane.

"Oh no!" said Dolina, "you are not taking me into the
river again!" and she was going to dismount, when she realised that the bracelet was still on the horse. "Oh dear! I'd
better stay wherever it is," she said, and was terrified when
the horse entered the swirling waters. Deeper and deeper
went till it had to swim. Dolina was frightened, and
thankful when they reached the other side and she could
run after the rolling bracelet again.

"I hope it's not much further," she said, "for I am very,
very tired and hungry." Still the little gold circle ran
ahead, and Dolina kept watching it so that she did not
look up till it stopped again. Then what she saw took her
by surprise, for there was a huge rock almost the size of a
house. It was shaped like a top and looked as if it might
fall over and crush her any minute. The Spinning Rock! At
first, she did not dare to go near it, but she wanted to see
if it really did spin, so she went slowly towards it and gave
it a wee push with her finger, and it spun round and round
with a groaning sound. Gradually it got slower and stopped.
Dolina then noticed a small wooden peg on the stone,
which seemed to be pointing in a certain direction, and not
far from the stone was a hole. She felt so excited, this

101

must mean something! Perhaps the hole would contain a message about the lost sheep. She thrust her hand into the hole and felt a sharp pain, for it was full of small adders.

"I have been bitten by an adder," she said. "I shall probably die." But as she said it, the bracelet ran up her arm and squeezed it tight, and out of the two little holes that the adder's fangs had made, the poison came oozing. Now the bite would have no ill effects.

She spun the stone again and this time the peg pointed to a different place. There was another hole nearby, and Dolina put her hand in carefully to see what she could find. She drew it back just in time, before a swarm of wild bees buzzed about her. She was now feeling annoyed, wondering if it was all a nasty joke. But she lifted the golden bracelet and, hanging it on the wooden peg, gave the great stone another turn.

This time it spun so quickly and made such a strange noise, that she thought she had made a mistake and it would surely spin right off its point and crush her. But gradually it slowed down and stopped with the peg and bracelet pointing to a small mound. Quickly Dolina dug at the mound with her fingers. The soil was soft, so it was not long before she felt a leather bag, and lifting it, pulled the string which tied it and out fell hundreds and hundreds of golden coins! Happily she ran them through her fingers. She would be rich now, and need no longer serve her mean uncle. But because she was a kind girl, she thought, "I will buy him lots more sheep."

Going back was easy. The magic bracelet ran like a little gold wheel before her, and when they came to the river a new bridge had been built. She went first to the cave to look at the writing on the wall, but it was no longer there. Not so much as a scratch. So she went hurriedly back to the wood and there was Kenneth busy with the axe.

"Kenneth! Kenneth!" she shouted, "look what I've got!"

"The sheep?" he asked.

"No, but ——" and she emptied the bag of gold coins at his feet. "All because of my wonderful bracelet," she said, putting up her hand to pull it off her arm. But it wasn't there! It had disappeared. Dolina looked disappointed. Kenneth laughed.

"You can buy plenty of jewels now," he said.

"Perhaps the bracelet is wanted for someone else who needs it," said Dolina.

Dolina gave her uncle twenty more sheep, and she and Kenneth were married and built a nice house to live in.

20. The Peat Bog

Duncan's father was no longer alive, so his Uncle Robert helped his mother with the work of the croft. He managed the cattle, sowed and reaped the crops and cut the peat. Duncan helped with all this work, and today they were going up to the peat bog where Uncle Robert would cut the wet peat into square pieces with a special kind of spade and Duncan would set them up on end to dry in the sun and wind. They would be away all day, so they took a bundle of food — oatcakes and scones and a large jug of milk, for it was going to be a hot day.

They worked till midday and then sat down for a rest and a meal. Duncan noticed that there was a piece of the bog marked off with a circle of small white stones.

"What's that for?" he asked.

"Well," said his uncle, "one day when your father was working here, he started to cut where that circle of stones is, when a wee crooked man jumped out of the bog and ran round in a circle and shouted, 'Not here! Not here! Bad! Bad! Bad! My house! My house!' So your father marked off the circle with those stones and we have never cut peat from it."

"Is that all?" asked Duncan.

"Well, your father found next day, in the middle of the circle, a small bag."

"What was in it?" asked Duncan excitedly.

"Only a lot of rubbish."

"Where is the bag?"

"I don't know. Probably your mother has thrown it away. That tale of your father's was probably a lot of nonsense," said Robert. "It's probably much better peat than anywhere else. I'm going to cut it next." So, when they had finished their meal, he went inside the circle of small stones, and stripping the heather from the top, started to dig and slice with the special spade.

He had hardly got started, when up bobbed the wee bogman. "Bad! Bad!" he yelled, running round the circle. "Stop, or water will claim you," and then he disappeared.

"Oh Uncle, please stop," said Duncan.

"Nonsense," said Robert, and started to fling out the peat sods. But Duncan would not touch them, so his uncle stopped and went back to the usual cutting.

When they got home after the day's work, Duncan asked his mother, "Where is the bag the wee bogman gave Dad?"

"I don't know. There was only rubbish in it — but it may be at the back of the dresser drawer."

Duncan went to look at once. There seemed to be only the knives, spoons and forks and a few oddments, but right at the back he found a small, dirty-looking bag made of skin. He fetched it to the table and turned out its contents. Only a faded daisy flower, a bit of twig and a small round stone fell out. Duncan was disappointed, and stuffed them back into the bag, but at night, he took it to bed with him and put it under his pillow. He felt that there *ought* to be something magic about it. He wakened later in the night to see the queer-looking wee bogman standing by the bed. He was smiling at Duncan, and kept saying, "Keep it in your pocket always and dig." Then he gave a weird cackle of a laugh and disappeared.

"He's daft," thought Duncan, and went to sleep again. But all the same, he kept the bag always in his coat pocket.

The peat had to dry before it could be brought to the cottage for the fire. So the next work on the croft was to dig the ground for the potatoes to be planted.

"I shall give you a piece of ground for you to plant some potatoes of your own," said his uncle. So Duncan dug and planted his own potatoes.

One day in the autumn, his uncle went out fishing, leaving Duncan to herd the cows. There came a great storm and Duncan put the cattle to a sheltered glen before he rushed home to see that his mother and the house were safe. The storm had swept some of the thatch off the roof and knocked down part of the byre, buckets and bits of trees were bashing about everywhere, and part of a hay-stack was blown into the sea. His mother kept looking to the shore.

"Surely your Uncle Robert will have been able to take shelter with the boat," she said anxiously, but night came and no boat arrived. Days passed, and there was no word of Uncle Robert.

After a week, they heard that wreckage had been washed up on an island, but no body had been found, and they realised that Robert must be drowned.

"That's what the wee bogman meant when he said to Uncle Robert, 'Water will claim you'. I will never work that part of the bog," said Duncan. Duncan's mother wept.

"What shall we do without Robert?" she cried.

"I will do the work, Mother."

"Bless you, my son, but that is impossible. If only we had enough money to hire a man to help you. But we haven't."

It was now time to lift the potatoes, and Duncan went first to his own plot. He was surprised to see a small mound near it, covered with daisies. He had put his hand in his coat pocket to find a handkerchief to wipe his hands, when he felt the small bag. He took it out and looked at the faded daisy in his hand. It had one very large petal. He walked among the daisies on the mound, and noticed a daisy there that also had one large petal. This seemed extraordinary, so he took the piece of twig from the bag and there, growing out of the mound, was a little twig exactly like it. Then he looked at the stone from the bag, and was astonished to see one just like it lying on the mound. He was amazed to see a potato plant beside the stone, for he certainly hadn't planted a potato in such a silly place. He supposed he must have dropped one by accident and it had grown. Well, he would dig it up any-way, though he did not believe there would be any pota-toes. But there were! He could hardly believe it, but there were thirty potatoes on that one plant.

Duncan took them home to his mother for dinner that day. She started at once to peel the potatoes, and cutting the first one in half, the knife struck something hard. When she looked to see what was wrong, she caught sight of a glint of gold — and pulled out a golden coin.

"Duncan!" she shouted. "Come and see what I have found in a potato!" When he saw the coin, Duncan seized the knife and cut another potato. There was another gold coin! They laughed and shouted with joy as they cut, and found thirty gold coins!

And, though some people laughed at him, Duncan never cut inside the circle on the peat bog, and nor did any of the men who now helped Duncan with the work on the farm.